RALSTON SQUARELY FACED
THE ALIEN...

He tried to get past the P'torra again. The alien had wedged himself firmly into the narrow doorway, making escape almost impossible.

Ralston stepped back and quickly sized up the alien. He had fought enough of them in the Nex-P'torra war to have an appreciation for how strong and hardy they were. Once, he had blasted off both legs of a P'torra field officer. That hadn't killed him. He had followed the officer for almost twenty kilometers; along the way the P'torra had killed four different varieties of creature with his bare hands.

Ralston might respect them for their toughness, but he despised them for what they had done to the Nex — and what they continued to do on a half dozen other worlds.

"You think to slay me?" asked the P'torra...

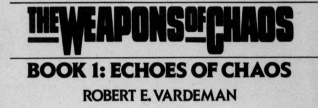

THE WEAPONS OF CHAOS

BOOK 1: ECHOES OF CHAOS

ROBERT E. VARDEMAN

BERKLEY BOOKS, NEW YORK

ECHOES OF CHAOS

A Berkley Book/published by arrangement with
the author

PRINTING HISTORY
Berkley edition/September 1986

ISBN: 0-425-09295-X

A BERKLEY BOOK® TM 757,375
Berkley Books are published by The Berkley Publishing Group,
200 Madison Avenue, New York, NY 10016.
The name "BERKLEY" and the stylized "B" with design are
trademarks belonging to Berkley Publishing Corporation.

PRINTED IN THE UNITED STATES OF AMERICA

To Roy Tackett

ONE

"WE ARE DYING." The gaunt, trembling figure turned and looked away from the others gathered around the long rectangular Table of Rules. Fordyne, advisor to the Council of State, statistician without peer, had never felt older and less able to deal with destiny. His burning amethyst eyes stared out the window of the towering Aerie and swept across the city stretched below him. From this height the chaos wasn't visible, but Fordyne knew it existed.

"You exaggerate," came the Chief of Rules' mocking voice. Fordyne's exhaustion vanished in a heady mixture of anger and frustration with such stubbornness. He spun, his embroidered chamber robes swirling around his lean frame.

"I do not." The fire in his reply took the Chief aback. Never had anyone spoken to the ruler of all civilization in such a manner. Politeness, if not duty, dictated only serene responses, measured tones, orderly emotions.

Fordyne had passed beyond accepted behavior. His world was dying around him and none of these fools believed!

"The facts are incontrovertible. Examine them. Have others you trust more do so. You will see." Anger faded, leaving only exhaustion—exhaustion and distress. He had worked hard for over three years, accumulating the evidence to support what his heart already had told him. The beige folders containing the results of the correlational study lay untouched in the center of the Table of Rules. No one at this meeting even dared open one and scan the first page abstract.

In their hearts they, too, knew what Fordyne had feared and had now shown true.

"Societal dynamics is a confusing issue, Fordyne," the Chief of Rules said, lounging back to nest in his feather-encrusted chair. He stared at the Council statistician. "You of all people know this. These . . . disturbances. They're random. No organized attempt is being made to overthrow us." The Chief snorted derisively. He laid one finger alongside his thick, hard nose to accentuate the point. "The last attempt to subvert a government is almost two hundred years in the past. Merno is stable. The country is stable." The Chief leaned forward, four-fingered hands gripping the edge of the table until the yellow-taloned tips turned white. "We are *all* stable."

"This madness has nothing to do with the toppling of governments by an organization," said Fordyne. "It—its only characteristic is disorganization."

"Talk sense. You're a scholar, not some giddy doomster on a park perch prophesying the return of feathered Larn, bringing his vengeance for our sins."

Fordyne noted several Councilors around the table stiffen at the mention of the mythical god. While the Chief of Rules scoffed at the ancient religion, Fordyne had learned that many—some in that room—had again embraced the old ways. They were less able than he to articulate their fears, and they reached out for solace, for explanations of why their secure nest/world was falling to pieces around them.

"Very well," Fordyne said, determination again rising within him. "A brief presentation. I trust its dryness will not unduly bore you."

Before the Chief could either approve or dismiss him, Fordyne reached into his robe and pulled forth a small projector. He aimed it at the far wall, and then stroked along its control surface. The window shutters closed, blocking off the deceptive serenity of Merno, the room lights dimmed, and a pale ruby beam stretched out over the surface of the wall. Tiny speckles set there burst into amorphous, colored life. To the eye came no scene; Fordyne's picture formed within the minds of all present.

"Fact: Accidental deaths have risen forty-six percent in the past seven years." The charts burned hotly into their brains. Many stirred uneasily but Fordyne had trapped them. They had to stay and witness the progression of evidence.

"Faulty control systems at General Guidance," muttered the Chief.

"Fact: Less than half of these deaths occurred during machine operation. Those that do have this profile indicate high probability, to the ninety-five percent confidence level, of operator error rather than machine malfunction."

"You're saying that all of these accidents are just that, accidents," pointed out the Chief. The others at the Table of Rules remained silent. They couldn't evade the numbers marching like a burning army through their brains, but they might dull their impact by concentrating on other, less disturbing ideas.

"The only malfunction, according to extensive autopsy evidence, is with the people." When the Chief said nothing to this, Fordyne pressed on. "Fact: Epilepsy has become epidemic among certain sectors of our population. It is my contention that the rise in accidental death is strongly linked to this factor."

"All these . . . freaks caused their own deaths? That makes them murderers," blurted out a Councilor.

Fordyne felt revulsion at this. Epileptics were not spoken of in polite society. This, in part, made it even more difficult to force the others to believe in the seriousness of the matter. They refused to stroke the pinfeather because of the proscribed affliction.

"It has become an epidemic," Fordyne repeated. He closed his eyes and calmed his rampaging emotions. To lose control, to clack your dental ridges wildly, insanely, to twitch and thrash about, to lose all civilized behavior seemed a fate worse than death. The stark embarrassment of such a seizure had, no doubt, caused hundreds—or by his numbers, thousands— of the afflicted to tread the only honorable path and kill themselves.

"Epidemics can be blunted, the disease cured. Such un-

sightly behavior is not induced like a viral infection," scoffed
another of the Councilors. "To say that such disgusting behavior
is induced—contagious!—denigrates all our medical science."

"I realize that it is difficult to speak of such things." Fordyne
squeezed his projector so tightly that the plastic began to warp.
He controlled himself and relaxed his grip. "But the facts will
not go away simply because we wish for some other cause."

"Wheeze!" The Chief whistled derisively through his dental
plate. "There's nothing wrong with this country, this world!
We've never been so prosperous, our people so at peace with
themselves and with their neighbors."

"Fact: Our population is in decline. The absolute number
of our people is beginning to drop."

"A mere anomaly," said the Chief.

"The birthrate fell to less than replacement fourteen years
ago. The latest flash figures from the medical division show
that the replacement figure has dropped below one." The projected image rustling through their brains contained sorrow,
funeral processions, infinite cold untouched by the pure flame
of rebirth.

"Explain."

"For every two deaths, there is less than one born to take
their place. The actual numbers." Fordyne stroked the side of
the controller. The ruby beam brightened as the images Fordyne
desired insinuated themselves into the others' heads. "For every
thousand deaths, there are only four hundred and eighty-nine
births."

"As I said, an anomaly. Time will ease this."

"There is more than an accelerating death rate, a declining
birth rate, and the . . . seizure numbers." Fordyne found himself
unable to even mention epilepsy. His hand shook harder and
fear rose within him, fear of personal shame. Nothing controlled his trembling, not even the illicit drugs he had been
using. "These are to be considered restricted data." The murmur
around the Table of Rules showed the Councilors' disapproval.
Secrecy solved nothing. And from whom would they keep such
knowledge? They had been at peace for well over a hundred
years, war only a vague, disturbing memory.

Fordyne pressed on. "Innovation and scientific discovery
are on the wane."

"Really, Fordyne, don't be absurd. You've carried this distasteful folly of yours far enough." The Chief of Rules rose and leaned forward on the table, knuckles bent under and supporting his weight. "I want to hear nothing more from you on this."

"Denying our trouble will not erase it," Fordyne said. "Look! Examine the figures. In the folders. Here!" He almost crushed the projector as he squeezed down hard on it. Columns of numbers, the correlational coefficients, the matrices laden with proof raced across the surface of their unwilling minds.

"Begone. We have other matters to deal with."

"As you will it, Chief." Fordyne bowed his head, both in deference to his leader's command and in defeat. He stroked the projector and a sigh of relief went around the Table of Rules. Once more they could deny without the interference of truth.

"They refused to listen?" Young Jerad stood staring at his instructor. Fordyne could only nod. "But the facts! The numbers! The high correlations!"

"They meant nothing to the Chief. Or to the others." Fordyne collapsed into an amorphous cloth cushion that threatened to swallow him whole. He almost wished that it would and put him out of his inner torment.

"But can't they *see* what is happening all around us?" Jerad hadn't learned patience. Fordyne closed his hot eyes and felt the welling wetness at the corners. Jerad would never learn. There wouldn't be enough time. Not for Jerad, not for anyone.

"They dismiss it all as anomaly, an unexpected singularity in the data. Such turnings in the number patterns have happened previously," Fordyne explained, more for the comfort of hearing his own voice than for any other reason. More softly he added, "But never with such impressive force."

"The results of my research," Jerad said, kneeling beside Fordyne. "Look!" The young statistician thrust out the folder. Fordyne laid his hand on the first page. Images flashed through his mind. He pulled his hand back and stared at his assistant.

"Yes," Jerad said, anticipating Fordyne's words. "One reason our research has deteriorated over the past few decades is irreproducibility. A classic experiment, even one as well-

documented as the light-speed determinators, give varying results with each new test. Even when the same instruments are
used."

This shocked even Fordyne, who had thought himself beyond surprise. "How?"

Jerad shook his head. Bright purple eyes blazed and his
lipless mouth pulled into a thin, determined line. "Cossia thinks
it might have something to do with the pass-by."

Fordyne frowned. What had been hailed fifty years earlier
as the greatest event in scientific history had proven to be
anticlimactic. Worse, the astronomers who had focused their
telescopes on the cometary object had been ridiculed when the
promised cosmic display of winter-sky-brightening coma had
failed to appear. It had set space research back a hundred years
and had, in Fordyne's mind, been responsible for the Council
canceling all attempts to reach either of the nearby planets.
Since those days, research funds had gone into geophysical
research, not astronomical. A race that had once soared on
wings doomed itself to remaining planetbound.

Fordyne sighed as he thought of missed opportunities. The
data to be accumulated upon reaching a near orbit of the planet
would have been immense. Even the geologists would have
benefited. He sighed again. It wasn't to be. The bulk of data
accumulated by the specialists in volcanoes defied mathematical analysis, being of a subjective nature. Lost opportunities.
So many. Too many.

He shook himself from the sad reverie, and asked of Jerad,
"What effect could the comet have had on us?"

"Cossia is unsure. She says it may have been a potent force
field, not unlike this electromagnetic field Illfon and the others
speak of. The comet may have cast its unseen net in front of
the planet, and we may have passed through it."

Fordyne did not call the theory far-fetched. What he had
presented to the Chief of Rules and the other Councilors counted
as far-fetched. Jerad merely theorized. A hypothesis and nothing more that might explain their data.

"Fordyne, your pallor . . ." Jerad stood, flapping his arms
futilely as if to take wing, as their ancient ancestors had done
at the first hint of confusion.

Fordyne tried to answer. He bit his tongue, felt the dental
plate severing the rock-hard appendage, drawing blood, chok-

ing him. He reached out and found himself trembling uncontrollably. Panic seized him. Fordyne flopped forward, thrashing about, knocking over tables laden with folders and drinking saucers.

"Help me," he croaked. Froth coated his lips and caked on his chin, hardening with dried blood. The world exploded in vivid, crazy colors and his eyes rolled up. Back arching, limbs beyond command, Fordyne dissolved into misery as the seizure fully possessed him.

"I am so ashamed," Jerad said, his head hanging low between his thin shoulders. Cossia's hand fluttered along a quaking arm. She stroked and soothed, as if Jerad were a fledgling who had fallen from his birthing nest.

"Fordyne is at peace. He counts numbers in a land beyond our understanding. He is happy."

Jerad turned stricken eyes to his friend. "You don't understand. He did not simply *die*. He was . . . taken."

Cossia pulled away.

"Yes," Jerad cried. "Like the others. He died in an"—he fought down his revulsion—"epileptic seizure."

"How awful! Such a great mathematician to be so dishonored."

"I did nothing for him." Jerad pleaded with Cossia for absolution. He did not find it in her amber eyes.

"You were his friend. While he lived, he conducted himself honorably. None can do more than Fordyne."

"I'd just told him of your theory concerning the pass-by."

They gazed at the funeral tree, now ablaze and consuming Fordyne's remains. They backed from the heat, waiting for the flames to die. In older times the trees had been real, but with the need to deal with thousands of deaths every year in the city alone, the funeral pyres had become increasingly symbolic. The trees were now of steel, and gas jets fueled the cleansing fires.

Jerad spun and stalked off, hardly trusting himself. His nose spasmed with the smell of Fordyne's cremation. Did that nose twitch signal the onset of a seizure? Or did he merely react to the odor of his mentor and friend's funeral? How could anyone tell in time to avoid dishonor?

Jerad shuddered.

Cossia's strides lengthened. She matched his bobbing gait perfectly. "We have no evidence, but much became confusing when the comet passed so close."

"Close?" Jerad shook his head. "It didn't even come near enough to the sun to leave a tail. What sort of comet is that?"

"My point, Jerad," she said, gripping his arm. "What if it left a gas in space and the planet swept through it? We might have been poisoned. The"—she swallowed and avoided naming their friend's affliction—"unfortunate disease might be curable, as many have suggested. We might find an antidote to this poison."

Jerad sucked in a deep lungful of air. Only the taint of Fordyne's passing marred the perfect spring day. Cool breezes blew off the ocean and pure rain would fall before sunset. He had always cherished the rain, enjoying its wetness against his thick hide. Jerad flexed one yellow hand, pushed back the sleeve of his robe and let the strong radiation from the sun bathe him.

"Why has no one detected this poison?" He didn't put into words his feeling that such a fine day put the lie to Cossia's claim. It felt *good* in the sun. She caught the sense of his emotions.

"We are dealing with problems beyond our understanding," she said. "Fordyne believed that nothing could be known unless it could be quantified. He failed. And from that we learn a valuable lesson. We must trust our instincts. Not in science but in emotion." She thumped her rounded chest. "Here lies the answer, not here." Cossia tapped her skull.

Jerad shrugged. Fordyne's death had left him stunned and peculiarly hollow within. Such dishonor for a researcher he had so admired.

"We must try. We must solve this problem or we will all end up stripped of life and dignity." Cossia glanced over one of her sloping shoulders. The heavenly flight crews had already prepared the death tree for another funeral. They had developed an efficient system for their task; too many left this world for the promise of clear skies and limitless flight.

"We must try," Jerad repeated listlessly. "Perhaps Dial's project is the answer."

Jerad doubted any answer to their problems existed, especially such a feather-headed one as Dial pursued.

• • •

The riots raged only a few blocks down the street. Cossia and Jerad peered out through a slit cut in the thatched wall of their refuge.

"It's no use, Cossia. They are caught in the throes of hysteria. The mob will destroy all Merno before dawn."

"If only we could understand. The answer is so close. I *feel* it!"

Jerad nodded. He, too, sensed their nearness to understanding. They had taken Fordyne's folders and gone over them, the numbers burning into their brains throughout long nights until they saw the clean, neat columns intruding into their dreams—and their nightmares. But they had studied these past two years since Fordyne had died in disgrace. To no avail.

The Chief of Rules had been assassinated. The Council's attempts to restore order had failed with the rise of one demagogue after another. Each subsequent fanatical leader brought civilization closer to the brink of dishonor. Any would-be leader who attempted to preserve discipline in the capital was not a leader for long. The mobs usually rebelled and destroyed them, as everything of worth was being destroyed.

Worst of all, even those such as Dial with his strange notion of escaping the planet had vanished in the ensuing years. All that remained to them was preserving what they could of their culture in hopes of a reborn society at some later, less chaotic, time.

A much later time.

"The fires burn closer," Jerad said, all emotion gone from his voice. Death no longer held the fascination and fear for him that it once had. To be gone from this world of illogic seemed a worthier goal than continued life.

"We can escape through the back," said Cossia, always the more tenacious of the two. "The vaults are still months away from completion. We need to work harder if we . . ." Her voice trailed off. Her large, mobile ears rotated. Cossia frowned. The sounds carried on the hot summer winds were confusing.

Then she *felt* what she feared most. Cossia spun and faced Jerad. Her friend, her lover, the most precious of all those left on this declining world jerked and twitched as if someone had attached wires to his limbs and sent electric charges surging. Jerad smashed hard against the thatched wall and fell to the

floor, arms windmilling out of control, purple eyes wide and
showing yellow sclera as vivid as his hide. Cossia ran to him,
but his strength startled her. With the ease of someone ten times
stronger, Jerad batted her away—and did not know that he did
so.

Cossia watched in horror as Jerad died from the epileptic
seizure, as so many others before him had done,

"The virulence," she said, her voice low and choked. She
had *felt* the onslaught, but it had taken Jerad so fast! Less than
a dozen frenzied heartbeats had passed from beginning until
death.

Jerad gave another death jerk, snapping his spine like a
dried twig. From past experiences, Cossia knew the twitchings
would continue for some time. Jerad had died following the
first seizure, but his body's resilience persisted.

Cossia looked at her own hands. They shook. Fear rose and
died within her. "Reaction," she said aloud. "Shock. Nothing
more." But Cossia knew she lied to herself. The epileptic convulsions that had killed Fordyne and Jerad would soon claim
her.

She *felt* it.

With the rioters only a dozen paces from the door of the
thatched house, Cossia burst into the street. She saw the de-
monic stares on the faces of the crowd, the expressions of lost
hope. Cossia almost despaired enough to join them in their fear
and frustration in burning down the city's most magnificent
edifices.

Cossia turned her misted eyes aloft to the majestic spire of
the Aerie where the Chief of Rules and his Council had once
met around the Table of Rules to decide the proper path for all
to tread. No longer. They had died in the riots, and now licking
tongues of orange flame sampled the base of the mighty building.

Cossia watched as the symbol of her world began to burn.
At first only the lower levels filled with bright oranges and
yellows. Then upper levels began belching black plumes of
smoke. As the fire quickly spread, the top floors crumbled and
the entire building's integrity was compromised.

The Aerie died, as did Cossia's world.

She let herself be carried away by the vortex of the crowd.
Slowly, Cossia worked her way into eddies and backwaters,

finally finding a deserted street leading into the countryside. Arms flapping in mock flight, she hurried along to the vaults. The others worked feverishly to complete the last of the accumulated displays, to seal them before the mobs thought about this final legacy and rebelled against informing future generations of their shame. But Cossia allowed herself a gut-wrenching doubt about the effectiveness of what she and Jerad and the others had done.

For whom were the vaults constructed? Cossia had seen the statistics compiled by Fordyne and his successors. This world died. There would be no survivors, no successors to carry on civilization.

Cossia *felt* it.

TWO

MICHAEL RALSTON FLOATED in the center of the University starship's main cabin, oblivious to all that went on around him, isolated by the sound-deadening effect of the lowered atmospheric pressure aboard ship. The trip to Alpha 3 hadn't been a long one by current standards, but it had worn on him. He didn't look forward to this dig; he expressed open hostility even to being assigned such a minor find when real work went begging on Vega 14 and Nuevo Seguro and Proteus 4.

He inhaled deeply, then exhaled slowly at the thought of Proteus. That should have been his. He'd been on the initial planetary survey that had located the ruins. A civilization older than mankind, only the second ever discovered that had possessed space travel—and possibly a stardrive—and waiting for the careful analysis and loving care he could lavish on it.

But it wasn't his. Alpha 3 was his while Velasquez got Proteus 4.

Ralston opened his eyes and noticed that the air currents caused him to drift slowly toward the wall section with the

13

chipped blue enamel. He extended arms and legs, slowing the small amount of rotation he'd developed. He started when he realized he wasn't alone in the cabin as he'd thought. Ralston faced a trim, small woman barely ten years younger.

He stared at her as if a million years separated them. He might be Leonore Disa's graduate advisor on this dig, but they had nothing in common. Ralston closed his eyes and went back into a self-pitying world. None of the students accompanying him shared his devotion to the field. Dilettantes, all of them. He had started on the flight with high hopes. He always did.

Nothing had come of them. The students were lackluster at best. All knew this wasn't the best expedition the University of Ilium had in space. That was Proteus. They were all second-rate students sent to a second-rate planet without sufficient equipment.

Or drive or skill, Ralston mentally added. His early attempts to establish any kind of rapport with the students had failed, and the professor had not been sufficiently motivated to pursue the matter. Better to drift off, lost in his own thoughts, his own pity.

Proteus should have been his! Damn campus politics!

Faint gabbling noises reached him, words altered by the lower than Novo Terra norm air pressure. Leonore Disa gestured for him to come closer. Ralston pulled in his arms and legs, increased rotation, and grabbed an elastic band stretched around the cabin. He collided hard, and then felt the band tighten and send him back across the room. With contemptuous ease, he came to a total stop beside the woman. She floundered a bit while turning simply. He took some small vindictive pleasure at her clumsiness. They had been in space for seven weeks, and the graduate student still hadn't mastered weightlessness.

"What is it?" Ralston asked.

"The pilot says we're about ready to shift out of stardrive." Leonore spoke louder than necessary. She also still misjudged hearing distances in the low pressure.

"Any guesses about how close to Alpha 3 we'll be?"

The incomprehension on her face told Ralston she had scant idea what he meant.

"How much longer till we get into orbit around Alpha 3?"

Leonore shrugged. Her brown eyes left Ralston's pale gray ones and focused somewhere behind the professor. He pulled in his legs and spun to see another graduate student enter. Ralston had even less respect for this one. If Leonore Disa, with her expensive implanted glowing jewelry plates and perfect coiffure seemed a dilettante, Yago de la Cruz proved even more of a dabbler. Ralston had no idea why the son of one of the wealthiest men on Novo Terra bothered pursuing a profession of dubious social standing, with few creature comforts and no promise for riches.

"What is it, Citizen de la Cruz?" he asked.

"The pilot says we're within a local A.U. of Alpha 3, *Doctor* Ralston. Shouldn't be more than another ten hours before orbit." Ralston watched Leonore Disa's face go from confusion to understanding as de la Cruz reported. She wasn't stupid, just ignorant, Ralston decided. Of de la Cruz, all he could say was that he didn't like the man or the sarcastic emphasis de la Cruz always placed on *Doctor* when addressing him.

"Good. Check out the equipment. Make certain we've got the monitoring station ready for grounding. While we're in parking orbit, we'll kick out the survey satellites." Caught up in enthusiasm over being able to work again, Ralston forgot his distaste for his assigned students and the paltry results likely on Alpha 3.

"At once, *Doctor* Ralston." De la Cruz misjudged his trajectory, bounced off the wall in an inept move, turned and glowered at Ralston, then shot through the door.

"He'll have a bruise off that," Ralston said, finding that he enjoyed the idea of de la Cruz battering himself.

"Doctor, may I ask a question?" Leonore's cheeks glowed a soft purple in counter to the lush pinks and flashing greens marching in strict geometric patterns along her hands and arms. He wondered if the implanted jewelry plates responded to the woman's emotions—some did—or if they could be programmed for random color display.

"Of course. That's why you're here. Consider this a giant classroom."

She frowned. He realized his bitter tone mirrored Yago de la Cruz's too closely.

"Sorry," he said, softer. "What is it?"

"We didn't come out of the shift very close to Alpha 3, did we? That's why we have to spend another ten hours getting into orbit."

"Actually, the pilot is to be commended on his navigation. Some commercial flights do a lot worse." Ralston looked around. The University of Ilium starship was hardly more than a space-going waste can. Reduced air pressure saved the cost of transporting expensive mass. Even the exterior walls were a light boron fiber composite hardly a centimeter thick—Ralston repressed a shudder at being so close to infinite space—and the cramped quarters had made him think that the University hadn't gone to any great expense hiring a pilot. In that, at least, he'd been wrong.

Traditionally and from preference, pilots interacted very little with their passengers. This one had proven no different, but Ralston had spoken to him twice in the seven weeks and had been impressed with his attention to detail and general knowledge of spacing. Ralston gave one over to the University for having the sense not to send out a novice pilot, even if this expedition accounted for little.

Coming within a local A.U. of their destination amounted to damned good navigation. While some might call it luck, Ralston knew better. The lesser pilots always erred on the side of increased distance. Shifting out of stardrive at less than this might indicate foolhardiness. One A.U. showed true skill, being neither too close nor too far from the planetary target.

"I've never been off Novo Terra before," she said. It hadn't been necessary for her to reveal this.

"There's not going to be much excitement," he told her.

"Not like there'd be on Proteus," Leonore said. He looked at her sharply. "Really, Dr. Ralston, we all know you wanted that dig."

"Alpha 3's not bad."

"It's going to be hard getting a good dissertation out of it," she said. Her frankness startled him. Ralston had maintained an aloofness from Leonore Disa and the others throughout the trip, contenting himself with the book he pretended to write. Whenever he had a few spare minutes he worked on it, but during seven weeks of unrelieved "spare minutes" he had done little more than jot down notes.

"That's one of the hazards in archaeology. You can't know what you'll find until you start digging."

"Where'd you do your dissertation?"

He smiled as he remembered. "A sweet find on Archænor

2. I was Benjamin Uzoma's student. Great instincts, he had. Great. One look at a site and he knew where the real stuff was. We spent seven standard months there."

"What did your research cover?" Leonore seemed genuinely interested. Ralston reflected briefly on the difference when he'd gone to school a mere ten years ago and the students now. He'd scoured the university library for every publication Uzoma had written, studied them, evaluated the quality of the work and decided he could learn much from such a man before even applying to the department. Leonore had just admitted she knew nothing of his background; Ralston doubted de la Cruz or any of the others had bothered to check into his publications, either.

That annoyed Ralston. The dissertation and the subsequent fourteen papers were his *life*.

"The natives had evolved into a 'social insect' culture. My paper dealt with the relationship between such a communal existence and its effect on architecture."

Leonore looked dreamy, as if thinking about the Novo Terra Gala Ball rather than archaeology. Then she surprised Ralston by saying, "Something like the Earth termite." Ralston waited for her to continue, to explain. "A few seem to have no function, but a dozen or more begin organizing into platoons and stacking pellets to the proper height and angle to make keystone arches."

"They manage to build very elaborate structures," Ralston said. "One or two can't, but a larger group seems to instinctively grasp complex relationships and know how to build in such a way to control the humidity and temperature."

"I remember reading that the termites worked together using chemical signals. I doubt the Archænor natives did, though. Too much acid in that atmosphere."

"You've read my dissertation," Ralston said. "That was my finding. They constructed on the basis of visual cues, being very sensitive to subtle changes in wavelength." He watched in growing appreciation as Leonore's jewelry plates flashed pastels. Someone with a good eye had programmed her plates; they heightened shadows on her cheeks, turning her face into something exotic rather than plain.

"I called it up from University files," Leonore admitted. "I was interested in seeing what your field of specialty was. We seemed to be stuck with one another."

"'Stuck' is a bit harsh." He wondered why he had withdrawn so on the trip. He might have been disappointed—crushed— that he'd been assigned to Alpha 3, but that didn't relieve him of his obligations as an instructor. He ought to have found out more about his students. As he had done with Uzoma, he should have investigated the strengths and weaknesses of his graduate assistants. It was, after all, what the University paid him to do.

"We're the lowest ranking students in the department," Leonore said without rancor. "And you haven't gotten tenure because of your involvement with the Nex."

Ralston stiffened. He hadn't realized anyone outside the department staff knew of his youthful windmill tilting.

"It must have been fascinating, being so close to a truly alien race. Is that what sparked your interest in archaeology?" Leonore's question came out innocent and almost ingenuous, but Ralston sensed a sharp intellect hiding behind the façade.

"Not really."

"They seem so . . . repulsive. The Nex, I mean." Her brown eyes speared him, demanding a substantive reply.

"I enlisted in their forces. I fought against the P'torra rather than for the Nex."

"Why?"

Ralston had asked himself the same question repeatedly. The humanoid P'torra had commanded human sympathy and aid. The reptilian, virtually boneless, formless Nex triggered only fear.

"If you don't understand it, oppose it," he said with a bleak smile. "That's the way most people responded to the Nex. I saw firsthand the atrocities done by the P'torra, though. Complete planets devastated. They used chemical and biological agents to depopulate four Nex-inhabited worlds."

"The war was started by the Nex," Leonore said. "They attacked the P'torra homeworld."

Ralston snorted. "I won't get into the politics of it. The Nex are alien in many ways and their views of both human and P'torra are skewed. They thought a quick strike at the homeworld would end the conflict. Instead, it only rallied support for the P'torra."

"They destroyed four worlds? The P'torra? I never heard that."

"Before war was declared, the P'torra killed two more. Six worlds turned into bacterial jungles. After the declaration of war, the Nex stopped them from harming any more of the planets, but the damage had been done."

"What did the P'torra gain? If the worlds are uninhabitable, they can't use them, either."

"A good point. Like most wars, this was fought for economic gain. The Nex were becoming too efficient in markets the P'torra coveted. The racial overtones came into play only after the P'torra saw how we could be manipulated by it. Societal shame over our own beginnings on Earth still run deep."

"After what happened on Earth, why didn't we rally around the Nex? A world destroyed is an awful loss, even if only the temperate zones on Earth are gone."

"Again, it's the Nex failure to understand warm-blooded psychology. I doubt one in a thousand citizens even know of the P'torra world killings." Ralston unconsciously distanced himself from Leonore, letting the lowered pressure isolate him again. Then he forced himself back within distance for easy hearing. Drifting in weightlessness and letting the bubble of silence formed a retreat to the womb. He might not like this dig or the promise held out by Alpha 3 or the students, but he had to make the best of it.

"I don't want to talk about that anymore. Get the others. We'll meet for a quick conference in, say, fifteen minutes."

"Very well, Doctor." Leonore Disa turned inexpertly, aimed herself for the door, and arrowed out, wobbling slightly around her major axis. All things considered, she did much better than de la Cruz had. And Ralston found himself glad for this, too.

Ralston smiled. He remembered his first time in weightlessness. He hadn't been able to eat and keep it down longer than a few minutes. But then the Nex food hadn't been palatable, either. Only when they shifted to a supply planet and he had the chance to buy four cases of peanut butter, a few chocolate bars and coffee from a black marketeer had he found adequate sustenance.

He made a wry face. To this day, he couldn't stand the sight of peanut butter. It had been all he'd lived on for over two months—that and the vile-tasting Nex supplements that gave nourishment and damned little else.

But Michael Ralston didn't regret his decision to fight with the Nex and against the more popular P'torra. Humankind hadn't been involved directly with the war—and had played an insignificant role in the final peace negotiations—but sympathies had been against any allying with the Nex.

He had been lucky Benjamin Uzoma hadn't carried such prejudices and had accepted him as a student. But even having such a noted archaeologist as an advisor and attending a school as prestigious as the University of Novo Terra did nothing to erase the resentment among his peers at Ilium. Velasquez got Proteus 4 and the first real chance at a spacefaring culture granted anyone in the department.

That should have been his! Ralston calmed himself as the seven graduate students began filtering into the room. What Leonore Disa had said about these being the lowliest in the department carried more than a hint of truth. Two of them Ralston suspected to be felons placed in a rehabilitation program. They spent their time huddled together, whispering behind cupped hands and furtively studying the others. He vowed to inventory his equipment before leaving the ship and after uncrating on Alpha 3.

Three more drifted in. He almost laughed aloud at that. Not only did they simply hang like sacks of dirty laundry, they went through their studies in the same lackluster fashion—they existed and little else.

De la Cruz and Leonore followed the others in.

Ralston studied both of them more closely, damning himself for not paying more attention earlier in the trip. Seven weeks had been wasted, as far as he was concerned. Of the pair, Leonore seemed the more enigmatic and promising as a student. He believed she had studied his dissertation closely but hadn't wanted to admit it. Some students asked questions to which they already knew the answers, thinking they could curry favor by looking bright. Leonore didn't seem that type. But what did drive her? While she was far from the top of the graduate crop, she wasn't simply squeaking by on the bottom like Asan and Lantalman.

He had to face the possibility that it had been his own aloofness that kept her from speaking up sooner.

Yago de la Cruz went hand-over-hand along one of the elastic ropes and positioned himself at the nominal "top" of the room. From this lofty perch, he glowered at the others.

Ralston had seen de la Cruz's type before. Spoiled rich bastard thrust into a world where money no longer bought his slightest whim. Ralston wondered how long it would be before de la Cruz offered him a bribe in return for his vote of approval before a dissertation committee.

Ralston slumped and folded himself into a loose sphere. Considering the probity of others in the archaeology department at Ilium, they might be amenable to a little extra money under the table. Even the department head might be bought for a substantial contribution in the form of unrestricted research grants. Ralston had to face the possibility that he alone in the department couldn't be bribed, that academic honesty meant something to him alone.

Always the rebel, Uzoma had said.

"Citizens," Ralston said, almost shouting to be heard, and pulling out from his comfortable position and pressing himself against a far wall, legs entwined in the elastic. "You've heard of the excellent navigation done by the pilot." Heads bobbed. He doubted many had heard or cared. For them this was little more than a vacation. In spite of his classes on field procedures he doubted any truly understood the work involved with a dig. That would change. Soon.

"We will orbit Alpha 3, launch our survey satellites and— yes, Citizen de la Cruz?"

"Why bother with new satellite recon?" the man demanded, his chin thrust out truculently. He reminded Ralston of a dog refusing to release an innocent victim. "We already have the preliminary ones. Their photos are better than we can take."

"I disagree. The exploration team that found Alpha 3 launched six satellites, most of them designed to detect life. Not the remnants of life," Ralston said. He shoved himself into the center of the room. He knew how a spider felt when it left the security of its web. With a quick grab, he caught a rope and found the appropriate spot to address his students. De la Cruz hung behind him, but Ralston ignored this. The other six floated where he could see them.

"An archaeologist has to be as much an electronics expert as a good scientist. We will be cut off from support and will need to repair our equipment. Who's taken the computer archaeology course?" All indicated that they had, but Ralston discounted any expertise since Pieter Nordon taught the course.

Nordon's technical abilities ran more to shovel than ultrasonic digger. Ralston knew Nordon hadn't wanted the course but had been forced into teaching it when it had come up on the seniority rotation. Nordon had been low man on the totem pole.

"The satellite will get us a better look at the ruins we're to explore." Ralston experienced a rush of enthusiasm. Back in the field! To be on a dig again, even an insignificant one, was a world better than lecturing or listening to dull seminars given by tenured members of the department. "Alpha 3's population died off approximately ten thousand standard years ago. That, hmmm, makes it close to ninety-two hundred local years ago."

"What killed the geeks off?" de la Cruz asked.

"The *population*, Citizen de la Cruz," Ralston said pointedly. "We will refer to the natives in the proper fashion. There wasn't any indication of the cause of decline by prelim reconnaissance. That's part of our job. The Alpha 3 natives weren't spacefaring, even to nearby planets, but their level of development might be very close. There will be enough information to go around," he finished.

No one looked excited, Ralston thought. Except—maybe—Leonore Disa. She was holding in her emotions, and only small muscle twitches were betraying her.

Leonore shifted when she noticed his direct gaze. She spoke up. "How do we go about choosing a topic for our dissertations?"

"Whatever interests you," Ralston said, surprised. Even such an uninspiring group of students ought to know better.

"Some of the other professors assign topics."

That didn't come as a shock. "I don't believe in such practices. Choose a topic of interest—and significant importance to the field of archaeology. You are expected to demonstrate imagination, innovation, and technical ability in how you pursue your research. I see no way to dictate a topic and then expect what must be the finest work of your career. Only when you're personally motivated, excited, can you possibly do this."

He looked around the small sphere of faces and shook his head. No excitement at being in the field. No thrill for potential discovery. Even worse, he detected no commitment to archaeology among his group. Why did any of them bother coming on the dig? Why bother putting in the long years needed to get a degree? They had guaranteed themselves a safe future when they had passed the tests and legally became citizens. Most of the students at Ilium came from wealthy families. What prestige did they find in a doctorate of archaeology? He hadn't found any.

"I can't say what we'll discover on the planet, but it won't conform to any preconceived notions. Each culture is distinct, with points of interest and real opportunity for advancing knowledge." Ralston wound down his pep talk. He found it hard to get too enthused over a pre-spaceflight planetary culture that had slipped into oblivion. Better to study a post-spaceflight world such as Proteus 4.

Damn Velasquez and his political maneuvers!

"You each have your duties. Go and get ready. We'll launch the survey satellites in four hours. By the time we're ready to ground, they ought to have good photos."

"How long will it take to analyze the photos and choose a site?" asked Leonore.

"With luck, we can get the largest city's ruins spotted and begin there within a day." His tone told them this conference had come to an end. They left awkwardly.

Ralston said nothing as Yago de la Cruz shot by, giving him a sour expression. Michael Ralston retreated to the isolation afforded by the center of the room and simply hung, lost in his own irresolute thoughts. Alpha 3 had to reveal something. He refused to waste precious time on a worthless planet.

His own mood darkened, though. No one at the University of Ilium was likely to give him a choice assignment, even if he did his best here. On Alpha 3 he'd be lucky to find anything worthy of a publication, anything more advanced than mud and firehardened sticks.

Damn!

THREE

MICHAEL RALSTON CRANED his head back until his neck developed a muscle spasm. He rubbed the spot but kept scanning the pitch black sky of Alpha 3 for the tiny, moving dots of his satellites.

The landing had gone smoothly, the shuttle setting them down less than a kilometer from the spot with the most prominent ruins. He had noticed Leonore Disa had been excited by the nearness to the solar physics research station, even if he hadn't been. The University facilities there were less than five kilometers away. But she hadn't allowed this to interfere with her work. She and Ralston had ended up doing most of the work while the others flittered about ineffectually. Since time had been a factor and the pilot had badgered them constantly from orbit for the return of the robot shuttle, Ralston hadn't driven the others as he might have.

Simply being grounded gave him renewed energy.

"There's one, Doctor," Leonore Disa said. He tried to follow the direction of her pointing finger. All he could look at was the pale orange and blue glow from the jewelry plates flashing just below the surface of her skin.

"Can you turn those damned things off?" he asked querulously. "Any light at all kills my night vision."

Ralston didn't see what the woman did but the plates blinked once before fading.

"Thank you. Now where did you spot it? Oh, that one." He frowned, his mind working over the orbits of the six satellites. "That's not one of ours. Too low in the sky."

"Might be one of the solar physics satellites," Leonore said.

Ralston controlled his anger at the mere mention of the University's solar physics station. No one had told him that another department had been on planet for three months. Something about the Alpha primary interested them. All he knew was that the physicist in charge had stopped by shortly after they'd grounded to warn him about higher than normal levels of solar radiation.

Ralston rubbed sunburned cheeks and brushed away the flaking skin. Their supplies hadn't included much in the way of sun screen, and he had let the students use most of what had been brought—the preliminary survey hadn't indicated it would be needed on a planet circling a G5 yellow-orange star. Even with a perigee of 0.82 standard A.U., Alpha Prime appeared less than four-fifths as large as the Earth's sun.

Ralston looked around the night-shrouded muddy plains where he and Leonore had come to pick up the latest intelligence from their photo satellite. In a way, Alpha 3 reminded him of Earth. It had been too many years since he'd been home—and for him, Earth would always be home. Novo Terra had become the center of human-dominated space after the wars had wiped out most of Earth's temperate zones, relegating it to a minor role among the stars, but Ralston felt that special bond between a man and his birthplace.

His only real regrets, other than the stupidity of the four-day nuclear exchange, were the losses of Catal Huyuk, the Ming Tombs, Puye and Chaco and Mesa Verde, and the entire Olduvai Gorge. This latter hadn't gone up in a radioactive cloud but had been destroyed by the huge numbers of people fleeing the higher latitudes. Ralston shifted from one foot to the other. The lewd sucking noise brought him back to the reality of Alpha 3 and the persistent rainstorms.

"Going to rain again," he muttered. Heavy, lead-bottomed clouds dotted the night sky, blocking off many of the almost-familiar constellations.

"Doesn't it ever stop? Why can't some of those hotshots over at Solar Base 1 do a better job of predicting the showers?" asked Leonore Disa. "That's supposed to be their field."

"Didn't know that," said Ralston, distracted. No one had told him anything about the solar physics research being done, and he didn't really care. That was out of his area of expertise. He had come to Alpha 3 to dig, and that's all he intended to do. Fraternizing with physicists didn't strike him as decent. They were too strange and would only divert him. When Justine Rasmussen had stopped by to greet them, it had wasted an hour.

"There! That's it." He swung around the hand-held half-meter parabolic dish, sighted through the axis optics, and placed the satellite on the cross hairs. A tiny red light flashed when he successfully locked on and received the recognition signal. Ralston flipped a tiny switch; a microburst went to the satellite and convinced the block circuits to release their precious information. In less than ten seconds Ralston had received two days' recon data.

He switched off the equipment and reslung it on his back. "That ought to do it. Wind and rain patterns as well as the radar images. Want to help me analyze it?"

"Sure, if you don't mind."

"Mind? You're out here to learn." Ralston smiled. "You're also along to do all the chores I detest. I *hate* poring over this type of data. I'd rather be at the bottom of a trench with an ultrasonic."

"That seems too dreary for words," Leonore said.

They sloughed their way across the plain and down into the lowlands, near a river where the largest ruins had been detected. Few walls extended above ground level, having been eroded away by centuries of wind and the incessant downpour. Every dig held its challenges. Alpha 3's seemed to be one of endurance. The rains ruined most carbon dating, forcing them to use other means to date the artifacts found.

"I read something once about Chinese water torture," Leonore said. "I think Muckup is it. All the time dripping on the top of my head. I swear, my brain cavity sounds like a drum."

Ralston sighed at the name the students had given the planet, tightening his own collar against the burgeoning rain. While picking up the satellite signal, it had been almost clear. Less than halfway back to camp a light mist had formed. Now gravid drops splattered heavily on them and gave birth to wet misery. Before they would reach shelter, they'd be drenched.

"Wear a hat," was all the advice he gave her.

Ralston and Leonore ducked under the low overhang and into his shelter. Rain beat a heavy tattoo against the plastic before running off to trenches he'd dug along the edges of the slope-roofed shelter. Ralston unslung the pack with the electronics and pulled out the small block circuit holding the data. He popped it into a viewer and focused against the back wall.

They studied frame after frame in silence, each taking notes and cross-referring what they saw. The computer automatically plotted isanemones and isotherms and detailed the information in a miniature map being developed at the lower side of the display. From this they might be able to determine the effects of erosion and better date the ruins. Ralston finished with one and flipped to the next, frowned, then reversed to bring the prior picture into sharper focus.

"What is it, Doctor?"

"Can't say for sure. Look at this. A good view of the city. Here's where we started with the cleaners. The computer's this dot. But what's all this? The lines and boxes?" He indicated the spot in the lower corner.

"That'd be about two kilometers away," Leonore said, working on the scaler. "How'd you take these shots?"

"Synthetic aperture radar. These aren't surface striations. It shows up off the major isanemones. They're just *under* the mud."

"Some structure that got buried. It could happen easily here." Leonore's tone indicated she saw nothing unusual in this discovery. Ralston had to admit the rains lent credence to such a theory.

But something that wouldn't go away kept flitting at the corners of his mind. Ralston finally pushed it aside and went on. In less than an hour, they had finished their mapping.

Leonore tapped her field computer and said, "Time to let it all digest."

"Time to get some sleep. I want to be up early in the morning to check out how the dig's going."

Leonore laughed lightly, the sound of silver chimes muffled by the patter of falling rain. "You'd work eighteen hours a day, if you could."

"Local day's only seventeen and a half," he said without thinking.

"I rest my case. Good night, Dr. Ralston."

"Good night, Citizen."

She left, a sudden rush of humid air entering to mark her passage. Ralston hardly noticed. He turned on the projector again and just stared at the patterns as if they might come alive and explain themselves to him. He fell asleep at the table, head on folded arms, dreaming of those hidden shapes.

"No, that's not the way!" he shouted. Ralston jumped down into the trench beside Asan. The graduate student backed off as if he'd been caught robbing the chancellor's wife of her family tiara. "Look. You've got to do this carefully, gently, as if you were making love to a sensitive woman."

His fingers stroked lovingly over the controls. The ultrasonic digger's pitch lowered, mellowed. Ralston guided the device forward millimeter by slow millimeter. Mud and grime vanished and a concrete foundation appeared. More quick touches produced a neat line of five green lights indicating that the machine had been programmed successfully and now worked at removing caked on grime and recording all data without destroying the object of study.

"There's no rush. If you had to do this by hand, it'd take months. The digger lets you go off and grab a nap now and again. You *do* have the alarm on it set?" Ralston saw Asan's furtive eye movements. That could mean only that the man knew nothing of what he did. Ralston shook his head and dropped into the mud-filled trench beside the digger. The graduate student hadn't bothered to set the alarm.

"How do you expect to find anything important?" Ralston asked. "You've got to use the equipment to the fullest."

"There's nothing of importance to find," came de la Cruz's sour words.

Ralston left Asan to ponder the error of his ways and vaulted out of the trench. His boots sank only a centimeter into the muck; they'd had a lucky two days without rain. He might have sunk in over the top of his boot, otherwise.

"Are you one of those rarities we see mentioned on the evening vidnews, Citizen de la Cruz?"

"What do you mean?" De la Cruz gave Ralston a suspicious look.

"A telepath. More precisely, a precognitive or a psychometrician, I believe the term is. You have a sense the rest of us poor mortals don't have?"

De la Cruz didn't answer.

"Can you tell us without equivocation that there's nothing worth finding at this site?"

"Nothing but foundations."

"But they are *big* foundations. This building towered, Citizen de la Cruz. It might have been the largest building on the planet. Surely that indicates the natives placed great importance on it. Maybe it was a governmental headquarters or a cathedral. What purpose did the building serve?"

De la Cruz shrugged.

"You don't know, Citizen de la Cruz?" Ralston asked with mock surprise. "Neither do I. But we're going to find out." Ralston studied the younger man, then motioned. "Come over here for a moment." He led de la Cruz away from the work site where the ultrasonic digger shook away more and more mud to reveal an interesting, but hardly unique, foundation.

"What is it, Doctor?"

"Your attitude, Citizen de la Cruz. Why are you on this dig? You barely do your share of the work. You display no interest at all concerning the natives that once lived here."

"Why should I?" de la Cruz blurted. "They're not important. There's nothing important on this mudball. Muckup's not going to get any of us the recognition we deserve."

"And what recognition is that?" asked Ralston. "What have you done to deserve any notice?"

"You don't like me because my family is rich. Richer than you'll ever be." A sneer crossed de la Cruz's swarthy face like a dark wave. "Admit it, Ralston, you hate me because you envy all the money I control."

"I may never be rich, but I have something you never will: satisfaction in my work. Even more to the point, I'm willing to work. You are lazy and willful and ..."

De la Cruz's face darkened even more. Ralston saw he had

pushed the student beyond his limit. Something about being judged worthless had touched off intense anger. Ralston barely ducked and backed away when the student swung a hard fist at his face.

De la Cruz recovered and came at Ralston—a mistake. Ralston felt descend over him the curious calm that he'd experienced each time before battle. Gone were the automated Nex weapons he'd become so expert with. But their intense hypnotic training remained. He deflected de la Cruz's fist, stepped inside, and slammed his fist down hard on the graduate assistant's neck. In the same motion, his knee came up to jolt into de la Cruz's groin.

Ralston blinked and came out of fighting mode. He hadn't realized the training still held such power over him. The last thing he'd wanted was to strike his student. His breath returned to normal. Ralston knelt, helping de la Cruz to sit upright.

"Sorry. Don't ever try anything like that again." De la Cruz jerked away and got to shaky feet. Ralston let the man go. He hadn't expected de la Cruz to physically assault him; he certainly hadn't expected his own quick reactions to produce such an outcome.

He turned to see Asan staring at him with appreciation. The man's eyes told Ralston that he approved.

"Why are *you* here?" Ralston asked, too loudly.

Asan shrugged. "Same as most of the others. Nowhere else to go."

Ralston started to snap back that he hadn't meant that. Before he spoke, he caught hold of his emotions, forced calm upon himself, and regained control.

"You are in a rehab program, aren't you?"

Asan nodded. Ralston knew he violated Novo Terra law and ethics; he asked what crime Asan had committed.

"Killed a few people who got in my way during a robbery."

Ralston barely understood. Killing for reasons of passion had never died out in any human culture, but thefts had become more and more automated over the centuries. To physically steal from another struck him as alien as the Nex. More so. They were supposed to be alien.

"Keep after the digger. Check to see if it hits anything its dig frequency might damage."

"Got an estimate on the building's height," Asan said.

"Must've been damn near ten stories tall. A lot for the way the rest were built: low, near the ground."

Ralston sat on the edge of the trench, feet dangling just above the muddy bottom. "That's strange," he said. "The natives were of avian descent. Flightless, possibly for most of their history, but very birdlike. Comes from the low gravity."

"You find a photo of the natives? Haven't found statues or any paintings. How do you know what they looked like?"

"Guesswork, right now. In a few weeks, we'll know for certain. Leonore found a skeleton—the first, actually. The natives were taller than we are. I suspect they had larger ears to compensate for the thinner atmosphere. Their bones were more fragile, more birdlike. Shoulders lead me to think they were birdlike, at any rate."

Asan gave his shrug and turned to clear the digger's sonic head of small twigs and rocky debris. Ralston heaved himself erect and began pacing through the city. Here and there the automated diggers worked to reveal the ruins of what must have been the largest city on Alpha 3. But it seemed wrong. Ralston had spent a good deal of his life wandering through burned-out cities, across plains hiding the secrets of the ages, and never had he gotten the feeling of such *wrongness*.

"Getting crazy," he said to himself. "Muckup's dead." He considered this. Archaeologists were hardly more than grave robbers, inspecting the dead and the belongings of the dead. Such a feeling of being surrounded by natives long gone ought to be normal.

It *was* natural to him after ten years of intense training as a scientist.

Alpha 3 held something more than a deceased race. Eyes unfocused, Ralston returned to his shelter, hardly noticing the rain pelting down harder and harder.

"Are you all right?" Leonore Disa asked.

"Hmm? What?" Ralston turned to stare at her. He hadn't heard the woman enter his shelter. Ralston looked past her and saw that the rain had stopped. For the time being, at least. He took a long drink from a flask, then silently offered her some.

Leonore made a face when she sampled it. She handed it back, asking, "What is that? Liquid lithium?"

"Bourbon."

"Why do you drink it? Tastes terrible."

"Maybe that's why. You must have some vices of your own. If not alcohol, then something else. It gives some limit to your existence, lets you put things into perspective. When you're stuck on a mudball like we are for at least a couple more months, this helps." He tipped the flask back and took another burning drink.

She pulled back her poncho and unfastened her blouse, exposing her midriff. A small silver plate gleamed.

"Oh," said Ralston, disappointed. "You're one of those."

"There's nothing wrong with recreational drugs," she said primly. "And the med-port makes it easier for a doctor if anything happens to me. I *hate* the idea of putting a needle into my arm."

"Use the air injectors."

"And leave a bruise?"

Ralston smiled at this. Bruises for someone with subcutaneously implanted jewelry plates would be an anathema.

"So you leak drugs into your system through that thing." He reached out and tapped the med-port. Leonore pulled away. "What do you use?"

"My privilege to use anything I want. I've been a citizen since I was eleven years old."

While this was several years younger than most who became full members of society—those that did at all—Ralston didn't think she was lying. There wasn't any reason to.

"You're hovering near the edge of ethanol poisoning for some reason," Leonore said. "Self-pity? You have a full measure of it. At least, when I 'port my drugs, I don't wallow in hating myself. They make me feel happy."

"*Feel* happy, not *be* happy," he said. Ralston knew better than to argue. Especially since she came too close to describing his state of mind. "I don't like being shunted off to this mudball—Muckup's such a fine name for it—but I intend to do the best I can."

Ralston frowned and took another drink. The bourbon burned his throat and puddled warmly in his belly, but he didn't taste it.

"Something's wrong with Alpha 3's archaeology," he said. "Just a sense. Everything we've uncovered so far indicates this city was destroyed by fires. Civil disorder is my guess. Riots.

To see an entire city of almost a million in flames!"

"You wish you'd been there?"

"Of course I do!" Ralston dropped the flask to the table and paced, hands locked behind his back. He studied her on every return of his nervous orbit. "There's no other way we can determine what really happened. All we do now is guess. We have only our intellect to piece the puzzle together."

"What do you think caused the rioting? War?"

"Not war," he said. "The destruction isn't organized enough. There's no systematic pattern as if an army marched through or aerial assaults took place. There didn't even seem to be an effort to bury the dead. That indicates . . ."

"Mass hysteria," cut in Leonore. "Or universal insanity."

"Yes," Ralston said, his mind abuzz with possibilities. "Mass insanity. As if they all went quite mad simultaneously."

"What could cause it?" the brunette woman asked. "There's never been a culture that declined worldwide for such a fantastic reason."

Ralston didn't answer. He turned back to the photo projected on the wall. The computer analysis had turned up nothing substantive, but his instincts told him that the neat rectangular patterns underground two kilometers south were important.

But why? What were they?

Muckup might provide a decent paper or two after all.

FOUR

"WE DO IT," Michael Ralston said. Leonore Disa looked up from the computer console, where she ran cross-checks on the architectural data they had uncovered using the ultrasonic digger.

"Do what?" The woman leaned back and pushed a vagrant strand of brown hair from her eyes. She hadn't activated the jewelry plates in Ralston's presence in almost a week. For his taste, that improved her looks, but he knew this was only a whimsical notion. They had all been in Alpha 3's rain too long. Leonore might have been a drowned rat with her damp hair and completely formless, soaked clothing.

"It's never good practice to jump about. Once you start excavation on one site, you make certain there's nothing more to be found before you move on." Ralston paced now, hands locked behind him. Every step he took rearranged the mud that had been tracked onto the floor of his shelter. A scant meter above his head, the fierce afternoon rain pounded harshly against the plastic roof and muffled his words. He might as well have been back aboard the University starship for the freedom of movement this planet afforded.

"You're thinking about the ruins to the south. You don't want to totally abandon this, do you?" She pointed to the photos with the superimposed grid pattern laid atop them. Each square carried its own identifying number. At the end of the day's excavation, one of them would remove the memory block from the ultrasonic digger and directly transfer the data into their main computer. The smallest item registered; nothing was overlooked.

While the excavation of the primary site had gone well enough, it hadn't revealed anything of real interest. Asan's earliest estimates of the building's original height had proven very accurate. Since then, only routine discoveries had been made.

Nothing worthy of a publication, much less a doctoral dissertation. No one in the camp had been happy over this, least of all Ralston.

"Never quit a project," he said, more to himself than to his graduate assistant. "That's when you're likeliest to miss the one important clue to a culture."

"But it wouldn't be out of the question to do a quick survey. Maybe using a couple EM probes? We don't have a proton magnetometer, but I might be able to juryrig something."

"Not that way," he said, settling into a chair. He faced the woman. Only with Leonore did he feel any need to explain his thoughts. The others did their jobs in a desultory fashion—automatons putting in their hours and nothing more. Even Yago de la Cruz had become more machine than human. Ralston almost wished he would show that spark of anger again that had caused the outburst and the abortive fight. Anything out of the ordinary broke the monotony—and Muckup's weather and former civilization had proven extremely tedious.

"Yeah, you're right. It might interfere with the solar physics equipment."

"What? Oh, them. I didn't even think of that. You're right."

"Some other reason?" Leonore's eyes unfocused as she thought. Ralston didn't interrupt her. Given a thread, she had proven herself able to follow it toward a logical conclusion. "The electromagnetic pulses might interfere with whatever's buried there. What do you think it is, Doctor?"

"I'm hoping it's a burial ground. We don't have any other spot marked off that is a more likely candidate for a cemetery. Hell, we've uncovered only a few decent skeletons. Most have decomposed badly, or were pretty much destroyed in death. Can't figure out how the planet's managed to keep up such steady rainstorms for so long. What analysis we've done doesn't show this recurring wet pattern prior to the decline."

"Sudden decline," Leonore said. "Less than two hundred years is the best estimate so far."

Ralston frowned. "Just a quick look at the southern site. A hand-held sonic cleaner, maybe some non-intrusive devices, a camera. Also an IR scanner to determine the boundaries and some of the walls, and to see if there're actually graves or not." He reached over and began rummaging through his equipment, getting what he needed for the short trip.

"Are you going to wait for the rain to stop?"

"It never stops. Or hadn't you noticed?" He smiled. "When's there going to be a better time? Want to come along?"

"Verd." Ralston winced at the slang. Leonore usually avoided such verbal bastardizations. She powered down the computer and peripherals, and then grabbed her poncho. With it on, she seemed even more formless. Ralston found himself wondering what she looked like when she went all out, dressed for a formal ball on Novo Terra.

He ducked out of the shelter and instantly regretted his decision to go exploring. The rain hammered at him with liquid, hard fists. Ralston blamed only himself for not being better prepared. The initial survey hadn't said anything about the incessant rains; they might stop during some other season. He had been unlucky enough to land with his seven students in the midst of a wet season when he had been expecting less rain and more sun.

If there was a dry season, he thought. He wasn't sure the original survey had been accurate. Even with the clouds, they were treated to more than expected solar radiation.

He and Leonore tramped southward for some time without conversation. Ralston finally asked, "Why are you here?"

"You said we were going to check out the ruins to the south." She stopped and peered at him through the curtain of rain. "Or did you have something more in mind? If you did, why didn't we stay in your shelter? It's not as wet there."

"That's not what I meant. Not at all." Ralston found himself tongue-tied in his confusion. His question had been directed toward an entirely different end, and Leonore had misinterpreted badly. Intentionally? He stopped, got his wits about him, then said, "Why did you come on the dig? What is it about this glamorous, fun-filled life that makes you want to be an archaeologist?" He wiped his forehead and sent a stream of cool water fanning out into the downpour. Droplet hit falling droplet, merged and tumbled to the muddy ground.

"Sorry, Doctor," Leonore said, not in the least contrite. "I mistook your intentions."

Had she? Ralston wondered. He pushed such thoughts from his mind. It was bad policy for a professor to become involved sexually with a student under any circumstance. That they had been away from Novo Terra for almost nine standard weeks only added to his frustration. Leonore Disa wasn't especially pretty, or even the type of woman he usually found attractive. But she was a woman. The only one on this ridiculous expedition.

"This isn't the life a socialite enjoys," he said.

"What makes you think I'm a socialite? The jewelry?" She shook her head. "I should have turned it off before the trip. Didn't even think about it since it's so much a part of me." They splashed through another fifty meters of mud puddles before Leonore continued. "I wanted away from my family."

"That's all? A vacation off planet could have achieved the same end—and much more comfortably."

"That'd be a temporary solution. I want something more permanent, a reason never to have to go back unless I choose."

"That upsetting being around your family? I don't have any. My parents died when I was young. They always told me to avoid the radiation zones. I did, they didn't."

"I'm sorry."

"So you're running away. Happy to run away to this?" Ralston made a sweeping motion. Rain fell in a steady stream off his arm. He quickly lowered it and shook free the water before it started soaking through. Even waterproofed, the material succeeded in becoming engorged with the rain.

"Actually, yes. I know the others don't enjoy this much, but I do."

"Asan and Lantalman are both rehabs. They've been so

heavily hypno'd there's no telling where they think they are—
or maybe they can't care."

"I heard about them being with us before we left Novo
Terra," the woman said. "A shame to send them out like this.
A shame to brain-burn anyone."

"That's the heart of the program, get felons into useful
professions."

Leonore snorted. In the humid weather, this sent tiny sil-
vered plumes of steam from her nostrils. "There's no spark of
humanity left in them. They can go through the motions, do
everything by rote, but how can they possibly be more than
average? All their initiative has been stripped away by drugs
and hypnosis."

"My feelings, too," Ralston admitted. "But the other students aren't that much different, and nobody's been tightening
the bolts in their skulls."

"For them, I can't speak. I want to establish a solid reputation for myself," Leonore said. "My mother says I'll come
running back, that I'll never be able to do anything she or my
father haven't plotted out in minute detail for me."

"I think she's wrong." Ralston stopped and looked at his
wristcom. It provided a distance estimate as well as an inertial
tracking fix if needed to return to camp. The tiny red arrow
pointed almost directly backward to show the location of the
main site. Ralston touched a stud on the side and got a green
arrow pointing obliquely left. "That direction, about fifty meters or so to the edge."

The rain diminished by the time the green arrow turned to
a small dot in the center of the wristcom display.

"This is it," Ralston said. The muddy flats appeared no
different from any other stretch they'd passed, but the imaging
radar had found the distinct outlines under the surface.

Ralston turned his small ultrasonic cleaner toward the ground
and pressed the switch. It hummed for ten seconds, then shut
down automatically. The mud had been blasted away in a small
trench, but nothing of importance lay at the bottom. Methodically Ralston began a crisscrossing until he found a rectangular
block.

"The corner?" asked Leonore. She had been following Ralston with the camera, ready to take a photo of anything uncovered. She trained the camera on the stone block.

"Maybe." Ralston took the camera from her and flipped on the IR viewfinder. Using this makeshift infrared detector to trace the buried wall for several meters, Ralston mapped out the buried structure. Then a large hotspot showed. He used the sonic whiskbroom again and unearthed a metal door.

"Looks copper-clad," Leonore said, running her fingernail along the edge and scraping away part of the green corrosion. He silently handed the camera back to Leonore, and she took pictures from several angles. "There's the lock." Her brown eyes turned questioningly to Ralston. Procedure dictated that they be more thorough with exterior investigation before opening any tomb. If sealed, they might have to pump out a few liters of trapped air for analysis before opening. A fiber optic probe would then be put into the chamber for a complete photo scan before they tried to open the door. Any number of methods might be employed. Ralston considered building an airtight room, evacuating it, and then opening the door so that no new gases would be introduced. Great care had to be taken to avoid introducing unwanted variables.

And then the real job would start. No datum could be taken for granted.

"It's been opened. Not too long ago, either," Ralston said, examining the lock. He gusted out pent-up breath in relief. Several days of tedious work could now be avoided. The air within the find would be the same as that outside. "The scratches around the catch—it's a simple one—aren't corroded as heavily. I find it hard to believe this dates back to the decline. Certainly, there've been natives opening it since then." His wristcom worked on the information gathered by a tiny probe Ralston passed close to the scratches and the lock.

Leonore peered over his shoulder. "Opened less than a thousand years ago?"

"Took a while for them to all die off, maybe. This might be a shelter."

"It might hold the reason for their sudden disappearance."

Neither spoke for long minutes, each lost in thought. Ralston knew that this tomb held their future on Alpha 3. Publications? Seldom did a solid reason for a culture's passing present itself. Mostly, archaeologists guessed, made up fanciful theories, spent long hours debating what no one could ever know for sure. This tomb might hold the definitive answer to Alpha 3's abrupt descent from pre-spaceflight civilization to complete oblivion.

Several good, solid papers could result because he'd followed his instincts. Ralston knew the same thought ran through Leonore's mind. A dissertation topic that would have the journals begging to publish it came along all too infrequently.

But the procedures for opening such a tomb had been worked out a thousand years back. The earliest archaeologists on Earth had known what to do. Schliemann. Mouhot.

"We can't open it," he said simply. "To spoil whatever's inside is too great a risk. We've got to do it carefully, recording every step of the way." Leonore nodded. Ralston smiled and added, "But we *can* make a few preliminary checks."

He pulled the probe, mounted at the tip of a slender fiber optic, from the side of his wristcom. Lowering the probe through the lock, working it around, he got a good view of the lock's innards. All the while, the wristcom recorded.

"Michael, look out!" cried Leonore.

Ralston jerked the probe back, but the tip caught just inside the rim of the lock. The mechanism had activated at even this innocuous touch. The door let out a moan like a dying man and began sliding sideways. A blast of fetid air struck Ralston in the face. He choked and turned from it. When he looked back, he saw only a dark, yawning cavity. The door had opened fully. Leonore took pictures, switching to an IR light and lens.

"I didn't think this would happen," Ralston said.

"But it did. Should we? I mean, nothing seems to have happened. No demons from the pits of hell have rushed up to devour us." Even as she spoke, she instinctively crossed herself. Ralston doubted she knew that she fell back on the comfort it gave her.

Ralston considered the possibility that Alpha 3 had died from a plague and that this, as a refuge for the few survivors, might be contaminated. Even now millions of viruses or berserk bacteria might be gnawing their way into his blood, taunting his T-cells and daring the leukocytes to resist. He shook that notion off as paranoid. Never had such a naturally occurring disease been found on another planet; even if they had become exposed, their bodies were ecologies where a disease had to find a niche. If too foreign, it wouldn't survive. If it fit in too well, their bodies, bolstered by the arm-numbing series of vaccinations they'd all taken prior to leaving Novo Terra, would fight successfully against intruders. For the first time, Ralston actually envied Leonore her med-port. He rubbed his arm and thought how painless it would be having the serum injected into the computer-driven box, then slowly pumped into the bloodstream.

Only on the Nex worlds had biological disasters happened—and this because of the P'torra meddling with one bacterium in the food chain. The planet deaths had taken years.

But the slim chance still existed: he and Leonore might have been exposed to a lethal disease. And he hadn't brought along an analyzer to check.

"Think your wristcom's good enough to gather the info we need?" the woman asked. Leonore peered down the steps into the vault, eager to go farther.

"We'd better close up and get back right away."

"I don't see how the mechanism operated," she said. She ran her fingers along the edge. "The probe inside the lock acted as a key. What mechanism lasts for ten thousand years? They must have been serious about whatever was placed here."

"It might not be that old. And if they wanted to protect whatever's below, why design the door to open so easily?"

"Didn't want to protect it from people, just the elements," Leonore guessed.

"Go back to camp," he said. "Get an analyzer and bring it here right away."

"Disease?" she asked. Ralston shrugged. Leonore backed from the opening, reluctant to abandon such a find. "I'll be back as fast as I can run."

"Don't slip and kill yourself in the mud," Ralston cautioned. "The analyzer would be hard to replace."

"But . . ." Leonore's sudden flare of temper faded when she saw he only joked. "I'll carry it back on a satin pillow. What service, right? Remember me in your paper."

"Co-authors," Ralston promised. He adjusted the wristcom to check on his body temperature and pulse rate. While his heart beat more rapidly than normal, no other vital sign appeared out of the ordinary. This meant nothing, but Ralston took it as a good sign that he hadn't gotten a faceful of exotic alien microbes. Only a complete blood chemistry would verify his gut-level feeling, though.

"It's starting to rain again," he said. "Better get going."

"It's always raining. Never stopped. Not really." Leonore paused and looked directly into his gray eyes. "Be careful." She held out the camera.

"I won't enter until we get the analyzer running."

Leonore's lips curled into what was almost a sneer. Her head bobbed up and down, then she turned and vanished through the gray wall of rain.

Ralston heaved a deep sigh. She knew him better than he knew himself. The lure of that black square proved too much. "Only a step or two," he said aloud.

He peered through the IR range finder on the camera and saw a long hallway extending due south from the foot of the stairs. At twenty meters the corridor T-branched, hinting at an extensive subterranean facility. Ralston pulled the fiber optic probe out as far as it would go, then descended another few steps until the door frame came level with his eyes. To one side he saw the mechanism, an elaborately encased set of mechanical gears and weights. This alone might tell much about the culture and its development.

But the corridor. That branching both left and right. No magnet pulled iron more strongly than this mystery drew Michael Ralston.

His wristcom beeped loudly, startling him. He glanced down and saw that he still had the body scan activated. His pulse rate had climbed well past norms from the excitement. Ralston turned off this function and let the full capacity of its tiny block circuit fill with data.

"This is wrong," he said softly, but he couldn't help himself. Ralston went down to the lowest step and peered into the darkness. The Stygian black thwarted his eyes, but through the IR lens he saw walls covered with intricately painted murals. If he'd left the wristcom monitoring his pulse, it would have beeped again. Ralston forced himself to calm.

He looked back up the stairs. Rain pelted through the door and dribbled down into the corridor. He shucked off his coat, used it to meticulously clean his boots of all the mud caked on them, and went back up the short stairway. A few minutes tinkering with the door mechanism permitted him to half close the door. The narrow opening he shielded with his coat to keep out the worst of the water.

"IR goggles. We'll need to get out the IR goggles," he

muttered. Dropping to hands and knees, Ralston began using the ultrasonic whiskbroom to brush the dust on the floor to one side. He made sure that the wristcom and sonic cleaner both recorded the depth of the dust before he moved it. Analysis of the dust could come later.

Centimeter by agonizing centimeter he cleaned a narrow path the length of the corridor to the juncture. Most of the work Ralston had done in semidarkness, using only the wan light entering the door. Now, to both right and left, he saw absolute darkness. Using the IR camera viewfinder, Ralston studied the floor, walls—and beyond.

"Eat your goddamned heart out, Velasquez!" Ralston crowed. "Proteus 4 is shit compared with this!"

Ralston hurriedly whisked a path along the right-hand corridor for a distance of ten meters, then stopped and stood. He cursed volubly, wishing for visible light. He peered through the IR viewfinder in stark amazement at what he saw. Slowly, he took one picture after another, knowing the visible spectrum would reveal even more when they got down into these catacombs with the proper photographic and recording equipment.

"I don't believe this!" he exclaimed, turning to his left. The corridor stretched far beyond the limited range of the IR camera. He took a few more pictures before retracing his path to the juncture, then going down the left-hand branch.

Ralston had to stop several times and control himself. He shook with excitement. He had always wondered how Howard Carter and Lord Carnarvon had felt on entering Tut's tomb. Or the sense of wonder Griegos had experienced seeing lofty, delicate spires of Vegan spider steel for the first time.

"Dr. Michael Lewis Ralston, explorer," he said proudly. Ralston had always thought he had a firm, pragmatic opinion of himself and his abilities. Now he found himself more than a bit awed by the discovery he'd made. "Damn, but this is *great!*" he exclaimed.

Another corridor, again vanishing beyond the limits of his infrared viewfinder, stretched to the right. This vault might extend for untold kilometers. This might be only the top level!

A scratching noise sounded behind him. Ralston didn't turn. He was too intent on taking in everything before him.

"Bring the analyzer over here, Leonore," he called. "And I hope you brought a couple more film blocks for the camera.

I don't think a thousand pictures will scratch the surface. This is great!"

The footsteps became more distinct now. The squishing sounds drew Ralston's attention. Leonore shouldn't be tracking in water and mud. Not into the find of the century.

"Leonore, clean off your—"

Ralston got no further. Blackness filled blackness as a heavy object smashed into the side of his head. He reeled, then slumped to the floor, unconscious.

FIVE

WAR DRUMS SOUNDED. It took Michael Ralston several seconds to realize that he hadn't been mysteriously transported back to a Nex war vessel, that the only pounding lay within his throbbing head. Ralston opened his eyes and thought he'd gone blind, then realized he still lay on the vault floor. Rolling over produced a new constellation of flaring stars in his head, but the pain subsided. To his relief, dim light shone from the direction of the opened door. The wet odor of fresh rain and the gentle *pat-pat-pat* as it fell reassured him he hadn't been trapped in this alien subterranean vault.

"Dr. Ralston? Are you there?"

"Leonore, inside. Be careful," he called. He instantly regretted the effort. Ralston reached back and touched the large, tender knot on his head. His fingers came away sticky with blood.

"You said you wouldn't go in," came the woman's disembodied voice. Ralston tried to understand what had happened to him. Someone had hit him from behind, but it wasn't Leonore.

At least he doubted it. She sounded both envious and disapproving. Nothing in her tone indicated anger—and not to the extent of physical assault.

Soft shuffling steps neared. Ralston heaved himself erect and swayed slightly. The dizziness and nausea passed before Leonore Disa rounded the corner. In one hand she held a small light. In the other she carried the analyzer.

"Are you all right?" she asked. Ralston thought the concern in her voice sounded too real to be feigned. He decided not to mention the attack.

"Of course. No reason to think otherwise, is there? Just because," he rushed on, not giving her a chance to speak, "your professor showed his moral and intellectual weakness doesn't mean anything's wrong. I don't think I disturbed anything."

"You tracked in mud," she said disapprovingly. Ralston peered at the large chunks of drying mud on the floor between them. Either Leonore had entered, hit him, retreated and then cleaned her boots before re-entering, or she hadn't been responsible.

"Thanks for not doing the same," he said. Her boots were spotlessly clean. The woman frowned and Ralston knew why. He, too, had cleaned his boots. She had to wonder who *had* been tracking in the mud.

Ralston wondered, too.

"We'll do a quick check, then seal up and evaluate the prelim data," he said. "After we get a better idea of what we've uncovered, then we can bring in the real equipment." His enthusiasm soared again. The knot on the side of his head still throbbed, but curiosity over their find erased any discomfort.

"Any need to analyze the dirt on the floor?" Leonore asked.

"Later. I want a good set of photos for these." He took the hand light from her and gave the lens a twist. The narrow cylinder of light expanded into a cone five meters wide at its base. One of the small side chambers lit up.

Leonore gasped. Even Ralston had to restrain his impulse to cry out. The scene in the first diorama looked *real*.

"Them. The natives of Alpha 3," Leonore said in a voice cracking with emotion. "They preserved themselves in a museum."

"Are they replicas? It doesn't look like they're embalmed," Ralston said, peering intently into the scene. Unlike most dioramas he was familiar with, this one had no restraining rail or glass partition. Two natives stood, a full head taller than Ralston's 190 centimeters. Their heads lacked hair or covering of any sort other than a close-cropped down; the most prominent features were the ears. They stuck out like radar dish horns.

"Mobile ears capable of independent movement, just as you surmised," Ralston said to Leonore. "Good work. You guessed a lot from the moldy corpses we've found."

"They look so . . . so peaceful," she said. She started to enter the diorama for a closer examination but Ralston restrained her. "Sorry," Leonore said. "Got too involved."

She took out the analyzer and turned it on. The various indicator lights flashed, and tiny beeps came from the guts of the machine as it began photographing, running tests of a dozen different kinds, recording everything, missing nothing.

"This must be the start of the exhibit," Ralston said. "These two are reaching out in greeting."

"Or the end of the exhibit," Leonore said. "They might be waving good-bye."

Ralston laughed. "It never pays to jump to conclusions. We are scientists and must follow strict procedure, even if we've done such a good job of ignoring it so far. Study everything, learn what we can, *then* come up with theories to explain it all."

"Do you think this is representative of the terrain?" Leonore asked. The ground under the natives' taloned feet looked nothing like the mud flats that covered so much of Alpha 3. "They don't appear to be products of a wet world—not like Muckup is now."

Ralston reluctantly pulled his attention from the first scene. He wanted it all—now! But there was so much to examine. He had to pick and choose. And be more alert than he had been earlier. Down the length of the corridor he saw particles of mud. Whoever had struck him had rushed on, perhaps performing a cursory examination of his own.

"Do a quick survey. Don't let the analyzer do more than take visual, IR and UV shots. We'll be more thorough later." Ralston left Leonore and went back down the corridor to the juncture. As he'd guessed, bits of mud marked where his assailant had moved down the other corridor. Ralston itched to do a full, immediate investigation of this wondrous find. Never had an intact museum been found, much less one depicting scenes of everyday life.

The scientific papers he'd get out of this would turn Velasquez green with envy!

"How many of these scenes do you want done?" Leonore asked, her voice distracted. She walked slowly down the center of the corridor, shining her hand flash into each tiny diorama to study it visually before using the analyzer.

"Let's break now. We can spend years giving this the study it deserves."

"Each one is more intricate than the prior one," she said, her mind obviously working over the ramifications of what they'd found. "Might give a complete picture of Alpha 3. A complete history!"

"They were definitely of avian ancestry," Ralston said. Then he tugged on Leonore's arm. "Come on. Let's seal up the door again to keep the water out. We'll want to build an entry portal, a small office to store our equipment and clean our boots. The last thing we want is to contaminate a major find."

"They're statues," Leonore said. Then she understood what Ralston had said. "Sorry. Just getting too involved."

"I know the feeling." He ushered her out, almost having to shove the graduate student ahead of him. They managed to get the copper-clad door pulled shut, but didn't allow the locking mechanism to operate. Ralston crammed his dirty jacket in the small crack to keep most of the moisture out. Loss of the jacket seemed a minuscule price to pay for such a tremendous find.

He tapped his wristcom, set the inertial mark so he could return directly to this spot, then started back to the primary camp site. With cold rainwater drenching him, the hammering storm isolating him with his own thoughts, he wondered why he'd been attacked.

"Leonore?"

"Yes?"

"Don't mention this to anyone else. Not yet. I want it to be a surprise."

She peered at him questioningly through the driving rain, but bobbed her head in agreement. The longer they kept this to themselves, the longer she had to think and formulate her own theories.

• • •

The rain slamming incessantly into the plastic roof of his shelter threatened Ralston's sanity. He had almost enjoyed the long, boring trip to Alpha 3 because of the isolation it afforded. He had always wondered about this seeming anomaly. The cramped conditions aboard a starship—any starship, not just the tiny bucket the University used—did not promote friendships. Rather, crew and passengers withdrew into themselves.

He'd heard it said that there were more mystics among starship crews than in any other segment of human population. That might not be so, but all the Buddhists he knew were spacers. They'd spend long hours in deep meditation rather than speak to one another.

Ralston wished for time and quiet and isolation for that kind of inner looking, for self-examination.

Perhaps he held within him the clue to the person who had assaulted him. Yago de la Cruz kept rising to the top of the possible list, but Ralston couldn't definitely eliminate Asan and Lantalman, both hypno-burned and drugged to eliminate their violent tendencies. He had no respect for the rehab psychologists and their always-changing techniques. A new grant sent them off meddling and hypothesizing into different corridors of a person's mind. During the war, he'd seen how the P'torra turned captives into mindless, drooling beasts before reimprinting them into loyal soldiers.

Ralston shuddered. He had to admit that he feared the mind tinkerings as much as he disapproved of removing a personality and remolding it, even for the dubious benefit it afforded society. And he had no idea how to judge if either Asan or Lantalman had managed to slip out of the bonds of their rehabilitation.

Ralston began to pace furiously like a caged animal. The sound of rain added a frenzied quality to his movements. Why did it have to be de la Cruz or either of the two rehabs? The remaining three—he still discounted Leonore—might have a grudge against him. He'd made it clear that none of them would be handed their degrees, that they'd have to work hard for them, that he expected only the highest quality work. The University of Ilium had a reputation as being the school for the indolent rich. Ralston equated this with laziness, both physical and mental. It still surprised him that none of the students had approached him with a bribe.

A lavish grant, from a parent's company, in exchange for favorable treatment. He knew it happened all the time. Ralston's anger mounted. He had been cheated out of the Proteus 4 expedition because of such underhanded dealings.

He snorted in disgust. Proteus 4 would be nothing compared to this find. Nothing!

Ralston began viewing the photos taken by the analyzer using IR. He had tramped through mud and rain, been hit on the head and it had been a full planetary day—seventeen and a half standard hours—since he'd slept. Ralston ought to have been dead on his feet.

He wasn't. His eyes shone as he studied the photos. Adrenaline pumped through his veins, and he knew he could go another planetary day before he slowed and his mind dulled with fatigue. The excitement of this find was worth that much.

At least.

Leonore Disa peered out into the storm raging across the plains. Jagged bolts of vivid green lightning leaped from cloud to cloud to produce a constant rolling of thunder. The rain drove down so hard that it caused mud to splash up waist high.

She pulled her poncho closer and stepped into the full force of the wind blowing in from the distant ocean. The only redeeming quality, as Leonore saw it, was the new warmth of changing seasons. They had landed on Muckup during early spring. The early rains after they had landed had been frigid, but no longer. The temperature hovered at a very warm 305 degrees K.

Leonore tightened the headband on her IR goggles and peered myopically into the storm. What had been the road to the main excavation site had vanished in the torrential downpour, but wavering red lines shown through the goggles gave her some idea where the road had been. She doggedly walked until she reached the spot where the ultrasonic digger continued on, oblivious to the weather.

Instinctively, Leonore checked it and made certain it functioned properly. Then she kept walking, past the ancient center of government, past the boundaries of the city, and farther into the muddy countryside. Only when she saw the heat shimmers of an approaching ground crawler did she stop.

She knew Nels drove using IR, too. The low-slung, track-driven transport ground to a noisy halt just a few meters away. The hatch opened, and she saw Nels Bernssen waving. Leonore hurried inside the vehicle, slamming the heavy metal door behind.

"Stop dripping on the rug," the big-boned, blond man said jokingly. Oblivious to her soaked clothing or his own injunction against getting the interior wet, he took her in his arms and kissed her.

"Whew," Leonore said, finally breaking off for air. "You'd think we hadn't seen each other in four months."

"Four months, three weeks, four days, and a few assorted seconds, each longer than a century."

Leonore held back a girlish giggle. She leaned over and kissed Nels Bernssen again.

"Stop that," she said, batting away his thick-fingered hand as it worked on her clothing fasteners. He stepped back and stared at her in surprise. "Unless you mean it."

"The crawler's got living quarters," Nels said. "Nice for one person, a bit cramped for two."

"How cramped?"

Nels guided Leonore around until they landed on the bed. He showed her how nice it could be in the compact machine.

Afterward, Leonore half lay atop Nels. She kissed him, then said, "I couldn't get away any sooner."

"A likely story. I know you, girl. The only woman in a camp of men. Horny graduate assistants. A lusty professor. You just couldn't find time for a poor, lonely post-doc trapped on the barren plains, staring forlornly at the stars, pining away for the woman he loves."

"Nels!"

"Sounded good while I was saying it," the man said, smiling broadly. They kissed again. "But I *did* miss you. You don't know how glad I was when you managed to get assigned here to Muckup instead of with—what was his name?"

"Velasquez," she said, sighing. "That was a hard decision for me, too."

"I know. He's supposed to be archaeology's shining star, isn't he? Turning down a spot with his expedition to come to a nothing planet like this had to be a disaster for your career." Nels stared into her brown eyes. Softly, he said, "Thank you."

"I love you," Leonore said.

Nels heaved a sigh and sat up in the tiny bunk. "We've got to get moving. I promised the boss lady I'd check up on the latest data collection. Supposed to be beamed down in less than an hour."

"In this weather?"

"Why not? We've got the antenna array working just fine. Outer ring of sleeve monopoles, inner ring of folded monopoles with a low band reflector screen."

"I'm sure you've got a nice antenna," Leonore said, "but I meant that the rain would kill your signal from the satellite."

"That's why we used an omnidirectional antenna array. The damned absorption from the water is too much for us around 14 gigahertz without a lot of fancy massaging."

Leonore nodded. "We use a hand-held transceiver and have to wait for clear nights."

"Nights," mumbled Nels. "Radiation is too much in the day and the rain kills the signal most other times. Hell of a planet." Nels Bernssen smiled and pulled Leonore close once more. "But even hell looks more bearable with you in it."

"Thanks a lot," Leonore said sarcastically. "This is the first time anyone's ever told me I'd decorate even a miserable place like Muckup." She tipped her head to one side and studied the physicist. "I guess that's as much of a compliment as I'm going to get from you."

"You know how us post-doc types are. All the time with our head in the clouds."

"*Everyone's* in the clouds here." The rain's hammering against the outside of the crawler didn't diminish its tempo. If anything, the storm worsened. The teravolt discharges of lightning cast an eerie light throughout the crawler's interior.

"And Justine will have my ass for lunch if I don't get moving. Got to collect. But you know I love it. Otherwise, why come to such a wonderful vacation spot?"

"Dr. Ralston met her when we landed. I don't think he likes her."

"Who does? But from what Justine said about your prof, he's the one with his head in the clouds. Or his nose is going that way. Is he always such a snob or was it Justine's charmingly obnoxious manner that burned him off?"

"He wasn't mad at her," Leonore said. "He's just not an easy man to know."

"Can't be much of a researcher," said Nels, getting dressed

in the cramped space. "He wouldn't have been sent to Muckup if he was. This is Satan's left asscheek for an archaeologist."

"That's not so!" Leonore flared, surprising herself. She had no real feeling for Michael Ralston, one way or the other. He tended to be aloof, churlish, self-centered and, even worse, self-pitying. But, dammit, he was *her* churlish advisor. She had seen flashes of true dedication to archaeology. Maybe even brilliance. The way he had been unable to restrain his enthusiasm over entering the vaults definitely showed more fire burned under his cold exterior than anyone thought.

"This isn't such a bad place," Leonore went on. "We've made what might be a major find."

"Sure. I saw the imaging radar pix. We took detailed shots before picking the spot for our base." Bernssen got the crawler in gear. They lurched off, mud flying in all directions. He flipped on the electrostatic shield to keep the worst off the forward window. When that didn't work, he cursed and started the mechanical wipers, which were only slightly more effective. The IR was good for finding warm bodies—like Leonore's— but impossible for driving in a storm. Bernssen preferred visual.

"You did? You should have offered them to us. It'd've saved us putting up our own satellites. The University has really slashed our budget to the bone. One landing pod—and the starship we came out in was ancient twenty years ago."

"It's a matter of funding. We've got a good chance at something *important*," Bernssen said. "The physics department had to fight off sponsors for us."

"Is that your antenna?" In spite of herself, Leonore felt anger rising. She was happy that Nels and the solar physics researchers got adequate funding. At the same time, it annoyed her that the archaeology department was tossed only well-gnawed bones for its projects, especially one as exciting as Ralston's find.

The omnidirectional antenna spread out over a full sixty meters of the muddy terrain. Leonore knew only the rudiments of com theory, but guessed that this array would pick up a dozen satellites simultaneously and multiplex the data into a station better equipped than anything her expedition had been offered.

She held back cold anger. They hadn't even been given some of the rudimentary devices like a proton magnetometer or a supervisor.

"Nice, isn't it?" Bernssen said proudly. He helped her from

the crawler. Together, sharing her poncho, they rushed to the door of the computer station. Once inside, Leonore's suspicions were realized. More had been spent on this single setup than for Ralston's entire expedition. Everywhere she looked rose large banks of state-of-the-art field computer gear.

"The room's air-conditioned," she said.

"Has to be. For the computers. We took the biggest available." Nels didn't seem to realize that all the University had provided Ralston were plastic huts and a single sanitary station. No heat, no air-conditioning, barely watertight shelters.

Leonore also saw that she'd lost Nels. His eyes locked on one terminal and he homed in as if on inertial guidance. He dropped heavily into a chair and began working on the data coming in from seven different satellites.

"We've got four in polar orbits, ten others in a variety of west-to-east configurations and three in geosynch orbits," he explained as he checked the flashing figures spit out by the computer. "The primary's never out of sight for us."

"Why so many satellites? The cost..."

"Cost doesn't count. I told you sponsors were tripping over each other's asses to fund us. We need all this and more if we want to monitor continuously."

Nels Bernssen's voice trailed off as another satellite spat out its data in a quick burst; the screen flashed and his attention centered on the work. Feeling neglected, but understanding his need to follow the experiments, Leonore wandered about. Most of the equipment performed functions totally alien to her. She'd never been especially good at physics, which was how she'd met Nels. He had offered to tutor her until she passed her basic courses in the subject.

She had passed, and his tutoring had turned to other, more intimate subjects.

"Glad you arranged to come out to Alpha, Leonore," the man said, not looking up from the terminal. "Not many women'd do that just to be with me."

"I'm glad now. More than just being with you, Nels. I thought I'd passed by a real chance on Proteus 4, but now I'm not so sure. We've got a big find. Maybe the biggest ever. It'll make a great dissertation. If I do it right, it'll establish me up there with Velasquez and maybe even Griegos."

"Damn!" Bernssen exclaimed, rocking back in his chair.

"What's wrong?"

"Things are moving faster than Justine expected. When was the starship supposed to be back for you?"

"Not for five months local."

"Damn," Nels repeated. He reached over and thumbed the communications unit mounted on the wall. "Justine, you there?"

"What is it, Nels?" came the project leader's voice.

"Just harvested the current crop from on high. Rayleigh-Taylor instability detected on the solar surface. Alternating hot and cold spots. Coronal activity mounting. The whole ball of wax. The computer's still working on it, but I'd say less than a hundred planetary days before burn-off."

Garbled static came from the speaker.

"Been talking to one of the grave robbers from over at the city," Nels went on. "Their relief's not due for a half year standard. Better send out a message packet to Novo Terra asking for an evac ship and get them the hell off before then."

"What!" cried Leonore. Bernssen motioned her to silence.

". . . damn radiation levels are rising, too. Cutting apart communication," came Justine's voice.

"You'll have to ask Rodrigo about that. He's the rad-man. All I do is solar hydrofluidics."

"Document everything. I'll get the packet starred off immediately, and I'll tell Stoneface he's got to vacate." Justine chuckled. "It's going to be fun kicking Ralston off planet. Teach him to be civil to his betters in the future."

"Nels, what's going on? We can't leave. We . . . we just found a site that'll turn the archaeology department around. It's a once-in-a-lifetime find!"

"Sorry, darling. Justine'll send the message back to the University. Ought to arrive in, oh, a week."

"A week!"

"Superdrive. Damned near nothing but stardrive engine, a tad of fuel, and a marble-sized compartment for the message. Doesn't take much to tell what's happening since the powers that be already know. Anyway, they'll dispatch another starship for you, and you'll be off planet in about two months." Bernssen's expression turned grim. "Even that might be cutting it fine."

"What's going on?" Leonore demanded.

"Darling, I'm sorry now that you came. Wait, don't get

mad. This isn't my doing." Nels smiled. "But what a chance! The primary's going nova."

Leonore had passed beyond anger. She simply stood and stared at him in disbelief.

"Really strange, too. This is a G5 yellow-orange. Shouldn't go nova, but everything's indicating it will. Soon."

"You knew the star was going to blow up?"

"We suspected, not knew. I've been mapping the surface of the star. The latest conformal mapping showed an oddity usually found only in rising magma plumes."

"The Rayleigh-whatever?"

"Rayleigh-Taylor instability. A density inversion. Heavier matter has come to the surface. Same phenomenon shows up in gas fingers escaping black holes."

"Your dissertation," Leonore said.

"Right. That's why they wanted me on this expedition. We're looking at a sun going nova. Up close, for the first time with full instrumentation, everything!"

"The radiation," Leonore said. "That's why we've all been sunburning so badly."

"You don't look too good with a peeling nose," said Nels. "Didn't Justine tell your prof to keep you out of the direct sunlight?" Nels shrugged it off. "That's just part of it. The instabilities are increasing. The solar mechanism is becoming increasingly upset. It started out following a familiar Bessel function, a zeroth order one. Simple stuff. The perturbations started creating flow pathways between the density layers. Now the oscillations in the corona are—" Words failed the physicist.

"We can't leave, Nels," pleaded Leonore. "Our discovery. What about it? The University wouldn't send us all the way to Alpha 3 unless they expected us to do our work to completion."

"They probably sent Ralston here to get him out of the way."

Leonore went cold inside. That carried the ring of truth. It was no secret that Michael Ralston was an embarrassment for the archaeology department. She had seen the others treat him as a pariah. Even she had been guilty of believing the stories before she'd gotten to know him better.

"Shouldn't have allowed anyone to come at all," Nels finished. "Especially you."

"What's the risk in staying?" Leonore asked.

Nels Bernssen looked as if she'd put the electrodes on his

ears and then turned on the current. "You're not thinking this through, Leonore. The primary in this system is going to explode, go nova, go *pop!* Nothing but superheated plasma will be left of Muckup and all the other planets. Nothing. Not a twig, not a pebble, not one single drop of that damned rain."

"We can't possibly get all our data in two months."

"Leonore," he said, taking her arms and shaking her, as if this might change her mind. She pulled away. "No one has ever witnessed a nova before. We've seen the after-effects— centuries later. We're dealing with a completely new set of data. G5s aren't supposed to blow up like this one's threatening to do. When I say the primary's going off in six months, I might be wrong. It might be half that."

"Or twice?"

"Stop it," Nels said angrily. "You and Ralston and the others are going to have to leave when the evac ship arrives. Staying any longer is stupid. Suicidal."

Leonore Disa had come all this way to be with her lover, but she'd found more on Alpha 3 than she'd intended. She took it as a personal affront that she wouldn't be allowed to study the vault and pry loose the answers to this planet's mysteries locked within.

"Get me back to the dig right now," she said. "We've got a lot of work to do."

SIX

MICHAEL RALSTON DIDN'T even hear Leonore enter his shelter. He bent over the hardcopy of a photo taken within the diorama, studying one segment with a magnifier.

"What happened to you?" the woman asked, startled at the size of the knot on the back of the professor's head. In the light, it showed as an ugly purple and green mountain of tender flesh.

Ralston jerked upright, knocking the magnifier to the floor. It lay there buzzing in protest. He switched it off before asking angrily, "Don't you ever knock before entering?"

"Sorry, Doctor," she said. "But what happened to your head? It looks as if you gave yourself a good rap." She reached out hesitantly. Ralston flinched away when her fingers brushed over the edge of the wound. "Let me tend to it."

"I'm all right. What do you want?"

Leonore dropped onto an uncomfortable plastic folding chair, and pulled it closer to the table. She hunched forward, hands clenching and unclenching.

"I've just been over at the solar physics site," she said.

Ralston's mind shifted from how to best investigate the intricacies of the problem posed by the dioramas to another type of problem. "Who'd you go over there to see?"

A hot flush rose in Leonore's cheeks. She hadn't thought her motives were that transparent, but why else would she willingly associate with researchers in the physics camp? They weren't archaeologists.

"Nels Bernssen. He's a post-doctoral worker for the University. We met about a year ago and . . ."

"Spare me the details," Ralston said impatiently. "I'm happy for you. May the two of you be happy forever and ever." The words came abruptly, a clear dismissal.

"Dr. Ralston, please. We've got to talk about this. What Nels found out tonight is important."

"All research is important."

His attitude began to annoy her. Ralston saw her mounting anger and added, "I'm sure Dr. Bernssen is very good at what he does. I'm also sure you are very proud of his accomplishments. It's just that our find today is foremost in my mind."

"It has a bearing on the find," she said. "Nels reported to his project leader . . ."

"Justine Rasmussen? She's the one I met when we first grounded. A garrulous person. All she wanted to do was talk. Didn't seem to notice we had a considerable amount of work to do then."

"Yes, her," Leonore rushed on. "Dr. Rasmussen has starred back a com packet requesting our immediate evacuation. Nels doesn't think it'll take more than two months for the starship to arrive."

"Ridiculous," snorted Ralston. "The ship just left. It'll be another few weeks before it'll even arrive back at Novo Terra. You know there's no way of communicating while a ship is shifting. Besides, it's too expensive to retrieve us this quickly."

"Nels said the University would send another immediately and damn the cost when they read Dr. Rasmussen's message. This system's primary is going nova."

Ralston sat and stared. The coldness within him spread, frosty fingers gripping at throat and heart and belly.

"No," he said. "You didn't understand this Nels. Physicists always talk in riddles and you simply missed his meaning. I read the survey reports. Alpha Prime is a G5, not too dissimilar from Earth's sun. They don't blow up, they collapse into white dwarves. I checked everything out about Muckup, too." Desperation entered his voice. He would *not* be denied his find! "I showed the planetary data to Estevez. He's the top-ranked xeno man at Ilium."

"The radiation levels are rising," said Leonore. "Nels found some sort of disturbance both in the star's corona and on the surface. He can't say exactly when Alpha Prime will explode, but he knows that it will eventually."

"That's it," said Ralston, a flood of relief washing over him. "He's talking in astronomical terms. That's like speaking with a geologist. They say 'soon' and they mean 'soon geologically' or 'soon in astronomical terms.' It might be a million years. For a star's evolution, that's fast."

"Nels means months. Maybe only days. Please, Doctor, call him. Or com Dr. Rasmussen and talk to her. I might have misunderstood, but I don't think so. Nels was too emphatic. We're going to lose not only the find but the entire planet."

"You told this Nels about the find?"

"I didn't describe it in any detail. He wouldn't have appreciated its importance even if I had. He's always been more interested in stability criteria." Leonore smiled wryly. "Sometimes, he's more interested in that than he is in me."

"Now I know you're exaggerating," said Ralston. Leonore's soft brown eyes shot wide open at the unexpected compliment. He smiled and pushed the hardcopy photos into an accordion folder. "I'll call Justine Rasmussen and see what's happening. It might not be as bad as your friend made it sound."

Ralston dragged out the small, battered com unit and fussed with it several minutes. Hissing and popping almost drowned out Rasmussen's reedy voice.

"Wanted to talk with you, Dr. Ralston," came the physicist's cracked reply.

"Why is the communication so bad?" Ralston shouted into the unit. "Shouldn't be this broken. Getting crosstalk from one of the other bands, too."

"We're being uplinked. I'm in orbit to align one of our optical telescopes." Hisses drowned out a sentence, then, "... Nels Bernssen is the expert. All I've seen substantiates his theory—his certainty now. I've already starred back the packet with a request for your evacuation. They'll have a starship here within two months to get you and your students off."

"What about your own researchers?"

"We've made plans to stay a bit longer. Our evac ship will follow yours by about a week, if all stays on schedule."

"When do you star back to Novo Terra, then?"

More static. Justine Rasmussen repeated. "We stay as long as radiation levels allow. We're hoping for as long as a year—but we're keeping the starship in orbit in case we have to run for it. Nels thinks we'll be close behind you on the way back to Novo Terra."

"We can do the same," insisted Ralston. "We can stay here, then leave when you do." Precious days might be all it would require to better examine the unique dioramas and the culture and history locked within their descriptive scenes.

"That's between you and University officials. We made our plans before we left Novo Terra. They might not want to go to the expense of leaving one of their starships in orbit for you."

"But they will for you?" Ralston's anger rose now. A career hung in the balance—careers, if he counted the dissertations his seven students could write on the Alpha 3 find. The responsibility Ralston felt for his students wasn't as great as it might have been, but it still existed. And he wouldn't be denied his chance at the greatest find since the Rosetta Stone. "There's no way they can force us to go back."

Ralston didn't have to hear Rasmussen's reply. Even though static tore apart her words, the sentiment came through clearly. The physicist told him in clipped, precise words he'd be destroyed professionally if he knowingly allowed any of his students to remain on a planet marked for vaporization.

But the find!

". . . talk in person," came the woman's parting words. A metallic click sounded, and all Ralston received was solar interference. He turned off the com unit.

"If we abandon the city site and concentrate on the dioramas," said Leonore, "we might be able to get a great deal done in two months. Not a complete workup, of course, but enough to save something. We'll be able to study the photos at leisure back at school."

Ralston hesitated telling her about being attacked within the alien museum. He thought it was one of the seven archaeology students, but new possibilities entered now. He couldn't restrict his suspicions to only the graduate students. It might be someone connected with Rasmussen's solar physics group, though this seemed farfetched.

The other possibility, as remote as it was, couldn't be discounted. An Alpha 3 native might still survive and stalk the ruins of its once lofty civilization.

"Let me consider our options," he said. "We'll keep working on the city until further notice. A day or two won't make a great deal of difference."

"But it might!" protested Leonore. "There's no way to estimate the extent of the displays without going down and mapping every turn in the tunnels. Just photographing it all might take months!"

"Don't mention this to anyone," Ralston said. "To anyone."

"But . . ."

Leonore Disa subsided when she saw her professor's determination in this matter. She spun and stomped from the shelter, vanishing into the curtain of rain plummeting from a treacherously clouded sky.

Ralston watched his graduate student leave, then turned back to the photos. Somehow, his concentration had fled. The more he stared into the magnifier, the less he saw.

Ralston wiped rain droplets from the lenses of the IR goggles. Stalking about to spy on his students struck him as absurd, yet he had to do it. To protect the sanctity of the find was important, but not of as great an importance as finding who had attacked him.

The rain prevented anyone not similarly equipped from seeing him. A quick scan of the compound showed no one else braving the elements. He moved quickly to the nearest shelter, the large one he had designated as a conference room. The pounding of rain destroyed all but the most muffled of words coming through the thin plastic walls. Ralston moved stealthily until he came to the back wall and a punchout spot where air conditioners were supposed to be mounted.

The University hadn't sent air conditioners or any other type of climate modifier. They'd sent nothing but the barest equipment necessary for survival. In a way, Ralston approved. This dig was supposed to provide experience for the seven graduate students. Living in shelters more suitable for a billionaire would do little to instill in them the need for innovation and the appreciation for detail.

Even if they failed in their attempt to gain their degrees, they would go out into Novo Terran society with a more acute appreciation of the luxuries afforded them.

Ralston pressed the IR goggles firmly against the thin plastic panel. Dim, wavering red shapes moved within. He made out three separate bodies before turning to press one ear against the wall.

The three students, Abeyta y Conejo, Fernandez and Butz, had been staying close together, and Ralston had spoken infrequently to them. On the starship he had ignored them totally after his feeble efforts to involve them in some sort of communication. Once grounded, he had given them their instructions and let them work unhindered. Now he wished he'd learned more about them—other than that they, too, were department rejects. The lowliest students were selected to accompany the Nex-loving Dr. Michael Lewis Ralston, he thought bitterly. While these three hadn't made any major mistakes on the dig, they hadn't distinguished themselves for brilliance or even great attention to detail, either. The best that might be said about them was that they put in their time and didn't complain too much.

Ralston shook his head. That sounded like an ancient prison sentence being fulfilled.

"... it's verd, I tell you," said Fernandez.

"She and that cloud of space gas?" scoffed Abeyta y Conejo. "She's too bonita for him."

"She's the only one who'll get a good topic, wait and see," insisted Fernandez. Ralston didn't have to guess at the topic being bandied about. "Just 'cause she's chinging him, she'll get the prize. That's the way it works. Verd."

"Who cares?" Ralston decided this had to be the third student, Butz, responding. "I'm here because my father said I gotta do something besides lying around Veral Beach and chinging all the good-looking muchas. Let them have their fun, as long as I get a degree. Then I can get back to the beaches where *I* can enjoy myself again."

After listening to the three curse Muckup's mud and perpetual rain, Ralston drifted away, heavy rain drowning the sounds of his boots sucking in the mud. Those three only verified what he'd suspected. Three rich kids forced into the University to get a degree and become "respectable." Too many of the rich on Novo Terra had fought and clawed their way to the top. Getting away from a burned-out cinder of an Earth had made them a hard breed. But that had been a generation back. For their children they wanted only the finest, the easiest, all that they'd lacked when growing up on Earth.

Novo Terra provided warm sun, soft breezes, temperate climate, fabulous beaches stretching for kilometers with eye-dazzling white sand. If anything, life on Novo Terra was too easy. Those who had fought so hard found their children drifting. That explained why so many pushed their offspring into graduate schools. Getting a doctorate was easier than cutting them off without any credit and forcing them to fend for themselves.

It did nothing to improve the quality of student work. Too many bought their degrees and appeased their parents that way.

Ralston knew that if he simply gave all three within that shelter a degree they'd be satisfied. None would care that it hadn't been earned legitimately. The professor smiled, water running away from the corners of his mouth, when he thought of Leonore Disa. In one respect, Abeyta y Conejo and the others were right. She *would* get the choicest project. He'd personally see to that.

Not because he was sleeping with her but because she of all the group shared some measure of his excitement for archaeology. Ralston believed that she would be in the field digging, struggling, sweating over shards and bits of steel to reconstruct entire civilizations whether she received her advanced degree or had to work as a technician. The work, the ineffable thrill of discovery, took precedence over status, real or imagined.

Ralston frowned. He knew Leonore came from a wealthy background like the others; what made her different? A pang of doubt assailed him. Were the three students right in thinking he harbored sexual fantasies about her?

Ralston pushed it from his mind. She wasn't that attractive a woman. What he felt might go beyond simple liking for a student—but it didn't go *that* much past.

The heavy rain and his lack of attention almost made him walk into the side of Asan's shelter. Ralston wiped the infrared lenses clear again. Through the thin plastic wall he could not make out whether there was one very warm body or two sitting side by side. Spying allowed him to hear Asan and Lantalman talking in their subdued, paranoid tones. They always spoke with protective hands over their mouths. He guessed this derived from time spent in a rehabilitation clinic where infractions of the rules merited far more punishment than did poor grades.

Ralston couldn't hear clearly anything that passed between the two rehabs.

He made his way through the sucking mud to Yago de la Cruz's shelter. One body inside. No sound. He moved on, hesitated when he saw Leonore's shelter, then continued into the night, strides lengthening until the ground seemed to evaporate beneath him. Ralston checked the inertial tracker in his wristcom until the green arrow turned into a dot and began blinking.

Through the IR goggles he saw the warm outline of the copper-clad door leading down to the alien museum. Carefully, he pulled out the jacket still stuffed in the crack between door and frame, pushed open the door, and went down into the corridor. Again using his coat, he cleaned his boots. He closed the door to keep out the rain and, satisfied that he didn't do undue harm to the hallway, turned and went deeper into the catacombs.

Ralston stopped and simply stared down the row of dioramas. Each held a slightly different scene. Each promised to give a clue to a different aspect of an alien culture.

Ralston swallowed hard as he mentally pictured the Alpha primary glowing whiter and hotter, expanding, the limits of its photosphere reaching out hungry tongues of plasma that eventually engulfed Alpha 3. The water began boiling off the planet's surface, then the atmosphere exploded into space. Before many more microseconds the planet itself began boiling—or would it simply sublimate? One second it spun through space as a muddy chunk, the next it was only superheated gas, a plasma cooling as it expanded to infinity. No matter how it occurred, boiling or sublimating, all this would be gone in the wink of an eye. The heritage of a lost race snuffed out by a berserk star.

"No!" he shouted. His single cry of negation echoed along the halls and finally died in the bowels of the exhibit.

He wouldn't let it happen. It couldn't! Such knowledge couldn't be lost forever. Ralston walked slowly down the corridor, came to a juncture, then reluctantly turned and retraced his steps. With his decision made to exploit this as vigorously as possible, using all seven of the graduate students, Ralston opened the copper door, exited into the driving rain, closed the door securely behind him, and followed the green arrow on the face of his wristcom back to camp. There'd be plenty of work to do in the morning.

Cold eyes filled with hate watched Ralston vanish into the downpour. With the archaeologist gone, he had nothing to stop him now. It proved only a matter of seconds to reopen the door leading to the treasure trove below.

SEVEN

DR. MICHAEL RALSTON DISAPPEARED into the heavily falling rain. Yago de la Cruz let his anger smolder as he waited several minutes before going to the copper door leading underground. He pulled out his professor's jacket and carelessly tossed it aside. De la Cruz descended into the alien museum again, smiling in grim recollection of how he had stalked Ralston here and struck him.

"Served the fool right," he muttered. De la Cruz made no attempt to be careful with his entry; his every step left behind a fresh cake of mud on the floor. All de la Cruz wanted was the big find, the discovery that would establish him in the field of archaeology. All his life he had been ridiculed by his family.

"Why don't you go into business?" they demanded. "Your father will finance it. Or your uncle. Or your aunt." Always they dunned him with becoming a success. *Their* success.

Everything Yago de la Cruz touched turned to dust. Three businesses had failed because of bad luck. How was he to know of so many laws governing import-export? That business had to fail when the government seized it. And who but his family could blame him when the orchid importer stupidly allowed the Terran rust blight to destroy the entire nursery? So what if de la Cruz hadn't kept the orchids in quarantine for the prescribed time? It had been the importer who had allowed tainted flowers to be starred to Novo Terra.

Of the third attempt, de la Cruz couldn't even bring himself to remember it. But the crushing failure hadn't been his fault, either. None of the chinging business disasters had been his fault.

The University of Ilium seemed his only refuge, his only chance for prominence and acceptance in his family's eyes.

"I can never be like my brother and sisters," de la Cruz said. The words echoed hollowly down the corridors. The sound finally died in one of the dioramas, swallowed by a distance both physical and temporal. "Arturo and Constance and Angelina are all in business. I'm not."

Anger grew within him again, a burning, ugly seed blossoming into hatred. How dare Ralston hide this discovery? It meant more than a simple paper to Yago de la Cruz. It meant freedom, it meant becoming his own man.

"If he won't give it to us, I'll *take* it," de la Cruz said, smirking now. He strutted up and down the narrow corridors, shining a small hand flash into each diorama. The slow progression in the scenes went unnoticed by the man. All he saw was opportunity and acceptance. A dissertation, yes, but more!

The University of Ilium officials might have rejected his application to assist Valasquez on Proteus, but after he delivered this find to them on a silver platter like Herod presenting the head of John the Baptist to Salome, they'd never deny him anything in the future.

De la Cruz crossed himself and muttered a quick prayer for success. What alien technology lay hidden here, waiting to be exploited? He might not have the business sense of his siblings, but a good, solid piece of hardware didn't require business.

Madre de Dios, he'd *hire* his family to market what he found!

De la Cruz turned a corner and explored deeper into the catacombs. Some corridors intersected while others ran a distance and came to a dead end. The graduate student frowned. Some sense ought to be made from the patterns. Only in that way would he know where to look first for the highest probability of finding something like Vegan spider steel or the fabulous refractory Lars Stormgren found in the devastated city on airless Prolix 11.

"Should be recording all this. Got to get it documented before Ralston." De la Cruz's smile turned even broader now. For whatever reason, Ralston hadn't done more than shoot a few photos and run the analyzer on the first strange scene set in its alcove. He hadn't ventured deep into the guts of this museum. The fool! Ralston might not have properly dated his photos or analysis, either.

"If he did, so what?" de la Cruz said to himself. "Photos can be lost. Analyzer findings can be erased." He rubbed a hand across his sunburned nose. With the high UV on this planet, a good case might be made for the destruction of many records by radiation. De la Cruz thought it would be a shame if Ralston carelessly pulled out the block circuits from his analyzer and left them out in the sunlight where irradiation destroyed the electronically encrypted data.

Stranger incidents had occurred on digs. De la Cruz knew. He'd studied the reports, seeking ways for a smart, ambitious man like himself to get ahead. After the boring seven weeks as they starred to Muckup, he counted himself an expert in all those methods. Not a single report in the starship's small library had gone unread.

For a moment, indecision struck de la Cruz. He shouldn't wander alone in the catacombs. Danger never entered his fantasies; de la Cruz worried that he might need a witness to "his" find. But which of the other graduate students would be the most amenable?

Certainly not that bitch Leonore Disa. She was chinging Ralston for her chance to study this underground museum—and it worked. *Doctor* Ralston had allowed her inside to use the analyzer. She would not suit de la Cruz's purposes. But he couldn't trust either of the rehabs. Who did? Their brains had been picked apart chemically, electrically, and mechanically and restructured in patterns known only to their rehabilitation psychologist. The other three graduate students seemed no better choices for what de la Cruz intended. Abeyta y Conejo had no ambition; he wouldn't fight his professor when Ralston challenged the validity—and priority—of de la Cruz's claim to this museum. Fernandez and Butz had no strength, no *coraje*.

De la Cruz resigned himself to working alone on this project. No other course presented itself. He thrust out his chest and strutted back and forth. With the proper altered records, he could claim all this for his own, even down to the last speck of the precious dust that Ralston seemed so solicitous of.

But the figures in the dioramas were the true find. Somewhere within them lay his future, his ticket to accolades!

He unslung a pack and pulled forth the cameras and portable analyzer he'd taken from the storage shelter. De la Cruz set up a few battery-powered xenon lights and turned the impenetrable murk day-bright. He switched off his handflash and slipped it into his pocket. Working as accurately as his eagerness allowed, de la Cruz set up the analyzer, slid in a fresh recording block and tapped a spurious date and time on the input keys. His claim now lay recorded a full two days prior to Ralston's blundering onto the doorway. Without diurnal light cycles, who was to say that this wasn't nine in the morning, local time? The analyzer, once started, ran continuously and no alteration of the start date was permitted without destroying the entire block circuit.

But de la Cruz had learned well. He need only fill up a block or two and his claim would be firmly established.

"This is the first diorama," he said, speaking so that the recorder built into the analyzer picked up his words. De la Cruz ignored it for further investigation. It had been the one Ralston had studied. Better to choose other, more interesting ones. That diorama held only two figures, both avian and neither posed in a dramatic fashion.

De la Cruz desired force in his photos, drive, drama. And, of course, the solid discovery of an alien technological gadget to exploit.

"The tenth diorama along the corridor holds several figures of interest." De la Cruz almost chortled when he saw one figure holding what might be a weapon. What would the Novo Terra Defense League pay for an alien weapon that couldn't be shielded against or circumvented?

De la Cruz placed the camera atop the analyzer and turned both to cover the diorama. He wanted his every move documented when he took the weapon from the birdman's hands. Stepping into the picture, the graduate student said, "I am now examining the artifact held by the ge—by the leftmost native."

De la Cruz took two quick steps into the diorama. For an instant, he felt as if he'd been returned to the freefall of a starship. The curious weightless sensation passed, not even leaving him with residual dizziness. But de la Cruz noted something peculiar.

"I . . . I smell burning organics," he said. "It might be tree leaves. Or hemp. And a small breeze blows warmly across my face. I . . . the sun is so bright. Not a cloud to be seen anywhere in the sky. Where did the rainstorms go?"

Confused, de la Cruz stood and stared. It had been night—and a storm had hurled downward its rain—when he'd entered the catacombs. Now he stood on a small rise looking out over a burning city. Flames licked upward to a brilliant sky, marring its azure perfection with greasy black plumes of smoke.

"You, traitor, halt!"

Startled, de la Cruz spun. He faced the native clutching the long-barreled weapon. The avian lifted the *sear* rifle. Tiny blue sparks marched along the top and sides of the barrel to sputter and spark at the muzzle.

"You, Wennord of Lost Aerie, have been convicted of crimes against the Nest. No more will we tolerate your rebellion. You might have destroyed our capital, but we, the rightful authority for this country, have caught and condemned you to death."

"Wait!" de la Cruz cried. He raised his hands to show he carried no weapons. The avian native aimed the *sear* rifle. De la Cruz stared into its black maw and saw tiny specks of red and white forming. The sparks coalesced into a miniature tornado that erupted from the muzzle. He felt himself thrown into the air, carried on gossamer wings, then dropped heavily.

De la Cruz screamed. He didn't want to die. It wasn't his fault! He knew nothing of this traitor Wennord. On hands and knees, de la Cruz pleaded with the native for mercy, to reconsider his dastardly crimes. But it had held such satisfaction for him to ignite the fuses that ultimately burned all of the capital.

He had conquered. Even in death, he, Wennord of Lost Aerie, had conquered by destroying what the tyrants held dearest!

De la Cruz slammed hard against a wall and fell prone. Sweating, heart pounding, he opened his eyes. It took several seconds for him to realize that he wasn't dead. The native hadn't fired the strange energy weapon.

And he wasn't Wennord of Lost Aerie.

The graduate student wiped the fear-sweat from his contorted face and sat trembling on the diorama floor. It had seemed so real. It *had* been real. He had walked into this chinging diorama and the natives had come alive and he'd been transported to a different world in the first rush of spring.

"Where'd it go?" he asked, his voice grating and cracked with emotion. He crossed himself twice and prayed for mercy from the aliens stalking him in the catacombs.

Where had they come from? He'd seen no trace of any bird-geek in the corridors.

On shaking legs, he stood and faced the figure with the weapon. He turned and looked at the companion figure, the one obviously being held prisoner by the armed avian. De la Cruz reached out to touch the energy rifle—the *sear* rifle the birdman had called it.

He jerked his hand back along the barrel, its static charge biting him.

"You might kill me," Wennord told him, angrily clacking his dental plates, "but that won't stop the rebellion. Look! Your precious capital city is in flames. *We* did that. You cannot halt the tides of progress. We will soar above your petty nestings!"

"Wennord," de la Cruz said, grinding his teeth and feeling the nervous tension along his forearms as fingers tightened on the energy weapon's trigger, "you are a traitor. It gives me great enjoyment to carry out my duty."

"May all your eggs break!" Wennord tried to bolt and run. De la Cruz whirled, lifted the cumbersome *sear* rifle and fired. The energy discharge rocked him back. Wennord blasted apart into a million burning fragments. Little enough punishment for defying the Chief of Rules and Council, de la Cruz thought.

He looked over his capital and knew that civilization had triumphed over the powers of anarchy this day. And he had been an important part of defending the Nest. His duty had been clear, and he would be given the highest honors in front of the Table of Rules.

He preened and began walking toward the inferno that was his capital . . . and stumbled over his analyzer, falling heavily to the corridor floor. De la Cruz jerked spastically, as if he'd awakened suddenly from a nightmare.

Hands trembling, de la Cruz grabbed the analyzer and used its familiar, comforting bulk to support himself in an attempt to sit upright. He looked back into the diorama; nothing within it had changed. One alien figure still clutched the rifle and menaced the other. Neither had shifted position by even a millimeter.

"Wennord the usurper," de la Cruz said. He licked his lips and swallowed hard. Moisture returned to his mouth. De la Cruz stood and stared. He knew what this scene depicted. No, he mentally corrected himself, he didn't know, he *knew*. As if every nuance had been burned into his brain, he *knew* the story of the last of the great insurrectionists and the man who had stopped him.

"I was there," de la Cruz said in awe. "I lived through it. I saw the pain, the destruction Wennord caused. But I know why he did it. He thought he was right. But he wasn't. I see it all!"

Awed by the impact of such knowledge, de la Cruz stared at the diorama's figures. He was galvanized into action by the sudden clutching fear that the analyzer hadn't been properly adjusted, that the camera had failed to record the bizarre scene. De la Cruz ripped off the protective plate on the analyzer and studied the red flashing numbers revealed on an interior instrumentation panel.

He heaved a sigh of relief. The analyzer had been running during his stint within the diorama. It had faithfully recorded everything, every whisper of radiation, every flash of light, the entire spectrum from UV to IR, and had sampled other frequencies along the way. Even com frequencies for microwave and shortwave had been monitored intermittently. He had it all locked with the block circuits of the analyzer! And the automatically recorded date made this discovery his and his alone!

De la Cruz almost re-entered the diorama to take the energy weapon from the avian's hand. Disorientation struck him again as he passed the plane formed by the front walls. He backed out, shaking like a leaf caught in a whirlwind. De la Cruz stood and stared until the tremors passed. He hefted the camera and analyzer and moved them along to the next diorama and the next and the next. He wanted to choose another which might give him the financially profitable discovery that would free him from familial guilt at not achieving all that they expected from a de la Cruz scion.

"The scenes show a definite progression in complexity," he recorded as he walked to another scene. "The first ones in this hall contained one or two figures, mostly without props. Later ones are packed with them. I am going to enter another diorama and take a sample of the material used to construct the statues."

De la Cruz experienced a thrill of possible victory in his search as he considered how these figures had endured at least ten thousand years. What material made up their bones and skin and turned them impervious to the passing eons?

De la Cruz entered an alcove with only four figures. He braced himself for the dizziness, but it didn't occur. Sure of himself, de la Cruz quickly stepped into the center of the figures and reached out with the analyzer's mobile probe. Using the device, he scanned the surfaces of the mannequin.

He jumped as an odd odor pervaded the scene. His nose wrinkled. He said, "I smell something. A cross between roses . . . and frying onions."

De la Cruz looked over his shoulder and caught a cold blast of air in the face. He blinked back tears and rubbed his eyes as he crossed himself.

"It's the event of the decade, I tell you," Blan said. "Think of it. When else in our history has a cometary object swept this close? If you fail to take full advantage of this opportunity, Zonnerg, all our grants will dry up. Believe it."

"Grants?" he asked stupidly.

"The Table of Rules frowns on missed chances to publicize their efforts as much as they do wasted funds," Blan said. His excitement obvious, the tall avian flapped his arms as if to take wing. "We can launch a platform, set it into orbit, and have a telescope on it to observe as the comet passes. It'll be so close the coma will stretch halfway out of the solar system."

De la Cruz nodded, slowly coming into agreement with his trusted colleague.

"You won't regret this, Zonnerg, you won't! The information from this comet will place us on the top perch for years."

"Launch it?" de la Cruz asked.

"Yes, launch it," Blan said, irritation entering his voice. "That funny thing the astro group has cobbled together will serve us well."

"We can go on from that," de la Cruz said, entering into the spirit of the discussion. "Why stop with a simple orbiting telescope? We can launch probes for the other planets. This comet can capture both the public's and the Council's imagination. Funds will pour into our nest."

"Yes, Zonnerg, yes!" cried Blan.

De la Cruz existed, his personality split between the avian astronomer Zonnerg and his own. As de la Cruz, he rejoiced. He had discovered spaceflight in this culture! Proteus 4 wasn't the only newly discovered post-spaceflight race. And this one was his discovery. He'd rank beside Velasquez before he'd finished.

Waves of staggering dizziness struck de la Cruz, but he recovered swiftly. He had expected it but still felt confusion and giddy disorientation after it passed. He heard himself—as Zonnerg—saying, "What went wrong?"

"The coma. It never developed. All our theories are as feathers on the wind," answered Blan.

"Comets are composed of frozen ammonia and other gases. It had to develop a tail," de la Cruz/Zonnerg protested. "We must have spectrographic readings to confirm this. We must!"

"The Council is angry at what they call a waste. The entire program has been canceled."

"But the planetary probe?"

"It, too," answered Blan, shaking his narrow head and blinking eyes of liquid amber, "has succumbed to public opinion. It will be many years before we can recover. Damn that comet! Why didn't it live up to our expectations?"

"We asked too much of it," de la Cruz answered. "There must be more to research than a single goal. We gained knowledge. The telescope is still in orbit. We can turn it on other objects. The stars! We can study them with Predario's new spectrum analyzer."

"My friend, it's not to be," Blan said sadly. "The Council has ordered the platform dismantled and returned to our southern hemisphere observatory. Space research is forbidden."

"But they can't. Not because of one comet!"

De la Cruz staggered from the diorama, still incensed at the failings of bureaucratic thinking. He stared directly into the lens of his camera; he heard the baleful *whir-whir-whir* as it took a photo every ten seconds. The analyzer continued to record on a wide variety of frequencies, missing nothing.

The student sat on the floor and cried. The entire planet's first tentative reach into space had been thwarted because of faulty theories concerning a comet. It was unfair!

De la Cruz shook himself free of Zonnerg's memories. For long minutes he simply stood and stared sightlessly. Then his own thoughts forced upward and replaced the void in his skull.

"Their history. It's all here," he said, jolted by the immensity of the discovery. There wasn't any need for a Rosetta Stone to decipher meaningless scribbles. He had only to walk into one of the dioramas and he'd be given a history lesson. He *knew* the lesson intimately after leaving. De la Cruz's experience carried far more weight than a simple book, too.

Their emotions, their motivations, all were his for the asking—for the living!

The audacity of the avians also impressed de la Cruz. "They have no fear in showing both sides. I was both the rebel Wennord *and* his executioner. I knew the reasons both acted as they did."

Never in all of human history had such a find been made. And it was his, his, all his!

De la Cruz could hardly restrain himself as he prowled the corridors. He guessed that a new student might enter the first diorama—the one Ralston had examined—and then progress to the next and the next and the next, learning as he went. By the time each diorama had been visited and fully experienced, a complete knowledge, both intellectual and emotional, of the planet would have been imparted.

De la Cruz stopped in front of a diorama near the end of the corridor. Only two figures crouched within. Without hesitation, de la Cruz stepped inside. He had learned to position himself in the same fashion as one of the avian mannequins—and he became Cossia.

"Are you all right, Jerad?" he heard himself asking. His body twitched and trembled oddly. It took several seconds for him to realize he was now a female in anguish over her lover.

"It's seized me again. I can't stop it. Oh, I love you, Cossia. I do!"

De la Cruz reflected on the strangeness of this diorama. The others had been scenes of obvious historical importance. A dying lover hardly qualified as being in the same rank as the death of a major space research program dooming the avians forever to a landlocked existence or the execution of the last traitor trying to overturn the planet's governing authority.

"Fordyne is gone. I follow in his distinguished steps." Jerad jerked about, his dental plates snapping shut so hard that pieces broke off.

De la Cruz/Cossia knelt beside her lover and stroked over a fleecy skull. "Don't worry, my love. The project is done. Dial is away on his star journey. And the vaults are filled. We will not perish without our memory wafting along the ages."

"This is the final record?" Jerad asked. His eyes had turned to dull orbs, fogged as if by cataracts.

"The final warning is being recorded now," Cossia said. Anger and frustration filled her. The unfairness to rob an entire planet of life filled de la Cruz/Cossia until he/she shook. "Zonnerg and Blan ought to have fought harder. We had to leave this planet. The comet. It caused our destruction."

"There's no other possibility," Jerad said. A massive convulsion struck him. The avian arched his back and jerked spastically, obviously dying. Cossia heard fragile bones snapping as the seizure took control of her lover.

Cossia stood. "Good-bye, dear Jerad. Good-bye, Fordyne and all the precious others. The end has come upon us. and we'll never know the reason. Only that the comet has brought the wrath of the ages upon us. But how?"

Cossia turned and straightened as courage firmed within her breast. De la Cruz was vaguely aware that he now faced the analyzer and camera, an actor performing for an unseen audience.

"The comet," he/she said, voice booming. "We are dead, but you, the finder of this vault containing our entire racial history, still have a chance. Use wisely what you have found here to solve the mystery of our death." He/she held out an imploring hand, then stumbled and fell to his/her knees.

De la Cruz recovered from the grip of the mental communication. His legs proved even weaker than before as he staggered out and braced himself against a wall. Within the diorama Cossia and Jerad still stood as they had for ten thousand years.

"They fled a riot-torn city—the capital," de la Cruz said, more to himself than for the analyzer. "The tall central building, the one we're scraping out the foundations on. That was the Aerie. The Table of Rules convened there. How magnificent it was! And their rulers. The Council and its Chief of Rules. They met on the uppermost floor of the Aerie to view the entire city."

The shakes hit de la Cruz—hard.

"Reaction," he panted when the quaking had passed. Yago de la Cruz stood on rubbery legs but smiled broadly. He had just gained an insight. There were things transcending mere wealth. His momentous discoveries in the dioramas would burn forever in the history and archaeology texts. Fame would be his!

All his!

EIGHT

MICHAEL RALSTON ASSEMBLED his small band of graduate students. He took a deep breath as if preparing for a lecture, then forced himself to relax. This wasn't a classroom on Novo Terra. They were in the field, and he'd made a discovery that would assure them all of a good professional future in archaeology.

Ralston only wished that more of them deserved what he was about to drop into their laps.

"Citizens, we're going to cease all attended digging on the city site. I want the automated data collection to proceed, but no longer will we stand and watch for the smallest artifact to be spat up by the ultrasonic digger."

Ralston paused for dramatic effect. It was lost on everyone. Leonore knew what he was going to announce, and the others didn't care.

"I've made what might be conservatively termed the discovery of the century." Ralston couldn't keep from grinning broadly now. He didn't care if they felt the same excitement

83

that he did. He had enough for them all!

"And if you're not conservative, you might want to call it the premier find of all time. I've uncovered an intact alien museum not two kilometers south of this site. The buried outlines showed up on the synthetic aperture radar photos taken right after we grounded, and Citizen Disa and I went out a few days ago to examine the site more closely. We opened a copper-clad door and found an extensive underground complex. While I've not explored it except to take a few preliminary photos, I'm sure these will excite you as much as they do me."

Ralston turned on the projector and began flashing the visual spectrum photos he and Leonore had taken of the dioramas.

He turned when Yago de la Cruz began chuckling.

"Citizen de la Cruz, is there something amusing about this? Do you find detailed depictions of the former inhabitants of Alpha 3 funny? Or are you so damned stupid that you don't understand what this means?" Ralston wouldn't let anyone belittle this find. It was big, it was *great*.

"Dr. Ralston, this isn't *your* discovery."

De la Cruz's mocking tone turned Ralston cold inside. "Explain yourself."

"Run this through the projector. And note the dates imprinted on each frame." De la Cruz dropped a block of ceramic film on the table. Ralston took it and held it in the palm of his hand. To Ralston, it felt colder than it actually was. He pulled out his ceramic photo block and inserted de la Cruz's.

Leonore Disa gasped when she saw the scenes that Ralston had just projected duplicated—and with earlier establishing dates. They showed that de la Cruz had taken the photos fully a week prior to her and Ralston's accidentally opening the copper-clad door.

"Dr. Ralston, we . . . " Ralston cut off her protests with an impatient gesture. His unwavering gray eyes locked squarely on Yago de la Cruz.

"Citizen de la Cruz, I want a word with you in private." Ralston fought to hold his anger in check. A single glance at the dates told him what de la Cruz had done to alter the time sequence. He had been the first human to enter the catacombs, not Yago de la Cruz.

And he now knew who had struck him.

"Doctor?" Leonore looked at him, worry lines wrinkling her forehead.

"I'll speak with you when I'm done with Citizen de la Cruz."

The others left, not comprehending the scene being played out before them. Ralston watched them go, wondering why the University hadn't sent along a flock of sheep. Those animals' genetic predisposition was to mindless behavior—and they were good at cropping grass and for providing mutton. These students showed the same wide-eyed stupidity and had none of a sheep's other redeeming values.

Leonore was the last to leave. She'd barely closed the plastic door behind her when Ralston swung around and faced de la Cruz. "You're not smart enough to doctor the records in such a way that they'll stand up if anyone really examines them."

"The analyzer I used is all the evidence I need that *I* found the geeks' museum." De la Cruz's smugness angered Ralston even more. He stepped back to keep from striking his student.

"It's not that easy. I'm sure you aren't smart enough to think of this on your own. What you weren't told, those aren't legal documents without the secondary time stamp."

"There's no such thing."

Ralston nodded grimly. "When the analyzer is constructed, an internal cesium clock is activated marking the planet of origin and time. It runs continuously, and the other clock, the one you set with a false date, is checked against it as an error-preventing service. It also provides protection against students cheating by date alteration, as you've done, Citizen de la Cruz."

"The trip here," de la Cruz cried. Sweat beaded his face. With sudden insight, Ralston understood that the panic he read came not from fear of being caught stealing another's rightful project, but from the impact of losing the accolades that would gain his family's respect. "We shifted in a starship. Starring here would destroy the reliability of any time stamping. General relativity. Space tensors."

Ralston shook his head. "Every shift is duly recorded—all automatic."

"It might not be working."

"The analyzer functioned properly, didn't it? Unless the cesium clock is running, nothing works. Some archaeologists have complained that their clocks were damaged and that they had to record everything in notebooks—by hand."

"That must have happened," de la Cruz blurted.

"Such documents are only valid when done holographically—and witnessed by two others."

"You're trying to steal my find!"

"No, Citizen de la Cruz, you're the thief."

"We'll let the head of the department decide." De la Cruz's dark eyes darted about, making him look more like a trapped animal than a serious scholar. "He'll decide in my favor."

"He won't. He can't. Not with the analyzer data showing that you misentered the date and presumably violated most of the tenets of careful archaeology with your meddling." Ralston's voice lowered. "You made another big mistake by revealing this ridiculous piracy. I know you entered the catacombs immediately after I did that first time and then attacked me."

"You'll never be able to prove it. You . . ." De la Cruz's words trailed off. His eyes widened and his mouth moved but only choked sounds issued forth. De la Cruz dropped to his knees and jerked violently, one arm flying out from his body so hard that he smashed into the table and sent it scooting across the shelter.

"What's wrong?" Ralston thought de la Cruz was faking this bizarre behavior. Insanity pleas were almost always accepted, especially from those who had starred from their home world only once. Something about dimension shifting adversely affected some people in a fashion similar to an allergy. De la Cruz might attempt such a ploy to preserve what little standing he had in the academic community.

Then Ralston changed his mind. De la Cruz was frothing at the mouth. No amount of acting could duplicate an epileptic seizure. The student's eyes rolled up until only the whites showed. Blood trickled from his lips; he had bitten his tongue.

"Leonore!" Ralston bellowed. He grabbed de la Cruz's shoulders, but the powerful convulsions threw the man free. Using hand-to-hand fighting grips he had learned during the war, Ralston succeeded in getting de la Cruz flat on the floor, face down and immobile.

"Michael, what are you doing to him?" Leonore stood in the doorway. All she could see was her professor pinning a struggling student to the floor.

"Get over here. Get something between his teeth. He's having a seizure of some kind. Damn!" As strong as he was and with as much skill as he'd applied the immobilizing hold, de la Cruz jerked free. Ralston had to release the grip or the graduate student would have ripped ligaments in both shoulders.

Ralston wrestled the writhing de la Cruz to immobility again. With one hand he grabbed a handful of hair and pulled back. This opened de la Cruz's jaws enough for Leonore to thrust a scrap of plastic between his teeth.

"His mouth is a mess," she said. "His tongue's all bloody. My lord!"

"Don't get sick on me," warned Ralston. "He needs attention right now. Get the automedic. I think de la Cruz's got a med-port. Find out what to inject and *do it!*"

De la Cruz's struggles had diminished until they were little more than powerful twitches. Ralston had no trouble holding the student down until Leonore returned with the portable medical unit. Putting a half nelson on de la Cruz, Ralston flipped the graduate student over onto his side. Leonore fumbled and opened de la Cruz's shirt to reveal the tiny silver plate in his belly.

"Attach it. Full analysis."

"That'll take too long. I . . . I started it reading Yago's med record. That'll be faster. This didn't just happen. God, why didn't they warn us?"

"My sentiments exactly," Ralston grated between clenched teeth. His own muscles ached from the strain of holding de la Cruz down. How did one fleshy, out-of-shape student generate so much power? Ralston had never seen an epileptic seizure before; such things were a rarity on Novo Terra. But he remembered his father talking about several seizure-prone friends back on Earth. Only this dim recollection had served him— and Yago de la Cruz—now.

"No history of seizures of any sort," Leonore said. Her voice rose to a shrillness that hinted panic.

"Start the automedic's analyzer. Not full scan, just emergency. Plug it in. Good," said Ralston, soothing her. Seeing a medical emergency of any sort lay far beyond everyday existence on Novo Terra and most other planets. "You do that a lot better than I could." His simple compliment steadied her. She flashed him a wan smile, then fumbled about to insert the connector into de la Cruz's med-port.

The automedic hummed and whirred. The hose that Leonore had connected began to buck and swing about when the machine decided on the proper type and dosage of medication and began pumping it into de la Cruz's bloodstream.

"Whew," Ralston said, lowering de la Cruz flat onto his

back. The student had gone limp with the influx of the drug. Ralston guessed the automedic had injected a tranquilizer.

He jumped when a siren went off and a bright red light flashed atop the machine.

"What's that?" asked Leonore.

"De la Cruz just died."

They stood and stared at the motionless body. Before dying, Yago de la Cruz had broken several bones. One compound fracture gleamed whitely where bone protruded from the flesh of his left arm. De la Cruz's face showed no peace in death, either. The seizure had ripped him apart, inside and out, physically and emotionally.

Ralston took a blanket out of a supply box and covered de la Cruz's face. It hid the graduate student's features, but somehow the formless mound mocked Ralston more than the contorted face.

"It's verd," Asan said with more fervor than Ralston had seen in the rehabilitated felon before. "They're going to brain-wipe you for certain. You'll end up a rehab." He didn't need to add "just like me" to scare Ralston.

"I didn't kill him. The automedic's report will verify that." Ralston tried not to sound too defensive. He hadn't done anything wrong, but he knew that appearances were more important in academic circles than actions.

Yago de la Cruz had been his graduate student during this expedition. His ward had died under mysterious circumstances. It hadn't been anyone's fault, but the archaeology department investigation committee and the chairman wouldn't care about that. They'd see this as a simple way of ridding themselves of Ralston. He had questioned policy one too many times, had tried to gain tenure in a system designed to reward obedience rather than brilliance, and had made damned few allies because of his stand for the Nex.

"He's right, Asan," Leonore spoke up. "The automedic shows some sort of massive neurological failure. It's too complicated for its simple programming, but Michael didn't cause de la Cruz's death. We all saw what happened."

Even a rehab like Asan caught the way Leonore now referred to her professor by his first name. Asan gave his neutral shrug that might mean anything. He turned and left.

"We've got to keep his body intact. Get it back to Novo Terra for an autopsy," said Ralston.

"We don't have the facilities," Leonore pointed out. "What's the usual procedure when someone dies in the field?"

"I don't know," Ralston admitted. "It's never happened to me—or anyone I've even heard of." The University of Ilium medical requirements for admission to a field program were as strict as any Ralston had ever seen; this was one of the few things done by the school that he approved of. Scanning the data on de la Cruz showed nothing to indicate why he had died in such agony.

"Do we bury him? Here?" The woman's voice threatened to break with emotion. None of them cared for Muckup. The constant rains, the thin atmosphere, the slight gravity and the muddy desolation all wore on them. Even if they hadn't liked de la Cruz, burying one of their own here seemed a travesty.

The war years came back to Ralston. The Nex hadn't been interested in retrieving their dead, but they had developed extensive battle zone facilities for recovering wounded. One of their pickup methods might be worthwhile to try. He had nothing to lose, after all—and de la Cruz wouldn't care.

Ralston went to the com unit and switched it on. The static wasn't as bad as it had been during earlier calls to the solar physics site.

"Dr. Justine Rasmussen, come in. This is Ralston, over."

Justine Rasmussen's voice barked out, loud and clear and annoyed. "What is it, Ralston? I'm very busy right now."

"We've had a medical emergency."

"Need our doctor?"

"Automated?" he asked.

"Automedic Model 23."

"That's the same as ours. University standard issue."

A long pause, then Rasmussen's worried question crackled over the speaker. "That unit'll handle just about anything. What's the problem? Did your unit break down?"

"One of my students died."

"You're not distilling your own, are you? You are serious about a fatality?"

"Quite serious. I need a large dewar flask and liquid nitrogen for cooling it."

"Corpse-sized dewar?" Justine Rasmussen caught on to Ralston's idea quickly. "Will fly it over to you within the hour. Need more than, say, fifty liters of liquid nitrogen?"

"That will be adequate until the starship comes. The body will be starred back to the University."

"You'll be going with it, won't you? Please remember what we spoke of earlier."

"I know, I know," Ralston said. "But it'll take almost two months for the starship to arrive. Plenty of time to make a decision about the rest of the expedition returning."

"The decision's been made," Rasmussen barked. "Alpha Prime *is* going nova. Our indications for it mount every day. There is no arguing with an exploding star, Doctor."

"Keep us posted. And thanks for the dewar."

Ralston flipped off the unit, then sat heavily in a sagging plastic chair. He wished he had a decent, comfortable one to sit in. He wished a lot of things. He hurt all over. Worst of all, a headache started behind his eyes. It felt as if someone kicked him with spiked boots.

"Michael?" came Leonore's hesitant voice. He opened his eyes and stared at her. "I . . . I went through Yago's things." She held out an analyzer block circuit. "I think this is his recording of all he did within the catacombs."

"He showed the camera shots," Ralston said, more tired than ever. "He really panicked when I mentioned the analyzer, so I knew he had one running. Go on, put that in. Let's see what the chinging son of a bitch did."

Together they watched. With every subsequent shot, their puzzlement grew. The analyzer showed de la Cruz walking into a diorama, then freeze in a pose for several minutes before shivering as if cold, then collapsing.

"Check the radiation readings," ordered Ralston.

"Nothing out of the ordinary. High static electricity readings, though. But that's nothing unusual. We've fought them ever since we landed."

"He shot these last night during the storm," Ralston said. "Static electricity levels aren't that high and might be caused by the lightning." He punched the rapid advance sequencer. They watched silently as de la Cruz invaded one after another of the dioramas. Each time he emerged, his smile broadened. But Ralston clearly saw de la Cruz's physical deterioration. At the end of the block's recording, de la Cruz trembled with an intensity just short of an outright epileptic event.

"Do you think he caught something by going into the dioramas? Some alien disease?" Leonore's voice had firmed. She was a scientist with a problem, and that precluded panic.

Ralston let her lean on that crutch—or whatever it was she depended on now to keep from screaming.

"You're thinking I might have loosed something ominous that had been penned up in the catacombs," he said.

"We, Michael. We were both there and we took the first photos."

"That's verd," he said, hating the slang even as he used it. "Our analyzer will verify that." He slammed his fist down hard against the table. The projector bounced and the picture shimmered. "Dammit, what happened to de la Cruz?"

"Poison?"

"Nothing I've come across indicates poison. Besides, the automedic would have found it quickly enough. It compared his current blood chemistry with his records. No, de la Cruz went into a diorama and something happened to him while he was inside. It wasn't poison or disease."

"Whatever occurred happened to him in each one," added Leonore. "The expression on his face when he left the first diorama changed from fear to . . . to triumph."

"Run a comparison of his block and ours." Ralston waited while the two blocks were checked by the computer. He punched in a request for only radiation and chemical comparisons. In less than a minute the negative answer flashed on the readout screen.

"Nothing unusual on either block. Both readings matched within a half percent."

"Nothing unusual at all, then," said Ralston. "I've been over our data several times. Nothing lethal indicated in it."

He rocked back in the chair and stared at the last image from de la Cruz's data as it shone against the far wall. De la Cruz stood with that shit-eating grin on his face, as if he had just conquered the universe. Behind him stood a pair of the avian native figures. Ralston's sharp eyes discerned minute differences in their bodies and faces. One might be male and the other female.

Other than this, he found nothing amiss. Certainly, he saw nothing fatal.

What had he loosed on this world? And did it matter, if Alpha Prime went nova?

Ralston had less than two months to discover the answer. Somehow, the thrill of his discovery had faded considerably. It had been replaced by a cold fear clutching at his guts.

NINE

"CAN YOU BLAME them, Michael?" asked Leonore Disa.

He could. But Ralston held down his temper. The past six weeks had been nothing less than hell. The students, except for Leonore, had refused to enter the underground museum, fearing a fate similar to de la Cruz's. Ralston stared out the shelter door at the bright silver dewar the solar physics group had given them. Plumes of condensation wreathed the large flask; inside lay Yago de la Cruz's frozen body. When the University starship arrived in a few days, the dewar and corpse would be the first items to go up.

Then Ralston and the students would follow. And his discovery would be lost for all time.

"I suppose it's only human nature," he said after a long pause. "They don't want to die like he did."

"They should have realized it was only a fluke, an accident of nature. Something made Yago susceptible to the messages. As long as they don't enter the dioramas, they'd be safe. If they'd only think it through!"

Ralston didn't argue with her. He wasn't as sure about the cause of de la Cruz's death as Leonore seemed. They had explored the dioramas far more carefully than de la Cruz. Starting with the first scene, they had spent a full week doing nothing but monitoring radiation from all frequencies. Along with this they had run a special analyzer with a surface acoustic wave sensor designed to pick up the most minute odors. Nothing unexpected had been found. No sign of danger.

That made the student's death all the more frustrating to explain.

A full seven days of observation—and no clue as to what had happened to de la Cruz. Ralston had then entered the diorama as they'd witnessed de la Cruz do. The surprise he'd felt at the telepathic communication, the sense of being transported back to a culture and time far beyond his wildest dreams at first had almost overcome the history lesson slipping across the edges of his mind. He had left the diorama quickly, Leonore recording everything.

Their most sensitive instruments detected no trace of the telepathic message. The analyzer, however, picked up the pheromones denoting Ralston's sudden fear, the sound of his heart hammering away, every physiological change he experienced as a result of the unexpected world forming within his head.

But the most careful examination by the automedic turned up no substantive neurological change.

Why had de la Cruz died when Ralston seemed unaffected?

Ralston had re-entered the first diorama and fully experienced the lesson. A change in orientation had produced a new and complementary version of the same lesson. And none of it impinged on their analyzer's block circuits.

He had been extremely careful and had denied Leonore her wish to experience the dioramas personally. If anyone took the risk of death, it would be Michael Ralston. But their slow progress down the corridor of dioramas, each scene taking a full three days to experience and for Ralston to record all that had happened, produced no physiological changes in the archaeologist.

Working steadily, doing two dioramas a week and using the seventh day to go over their data, he and Leonore had finished examining only ten. Dozens more lay ahead—and the final ones which might hold the secret to de la Cruz's death were more than a year away, if they continued on their current time-table.

"Nels called today," Leonore said. Ralston pulled out of his introspection.

"What did he have to say?"

"The surface disturbances on the sun have quieted."

Hope flared. "Then Alpha Prime isn't going to blow? We can stay and finish our work?"

Leonore shook her head. Ralston's hope died stillborn. "Nels doesn't understand the dynamics of the nova process, but he says their current theory is that it doesn't proceed in a linear fashion. There are odd spurts and surges, then a falling back into normal stellar behavior. But each leveling off comes at a higher and higher level, which makes new instabilities even worse. When they reach some unknown threshold, the star explodes."

"But this tailing off in instability gives us more time?" Ralston clutched at the slimmest hope now. The dioramas constituted a major discovery that must be exploited fully. Without the graduate students helping him and Leonore, recording the pertinent data had gone much too slowly. Any additional time allotted by the capricious star could be put to good use.

"Maybe. I don't know." Leonore smiled wryly. "Remember, I met Nels when he was a tutor—a tutor I needed to get through elementary physics. Why not ask him what this means? Or Dr. Rasmussen?"

Ralston hadn't gotten along well at all with Justine Rasmussen. Each subsequent call had become more brusque, colder. When she learned of de la Cruz's death and its possible cause, she had prohibited any social contact between the two groups. Of all the people affected, Nels Bernssen and Leonore Disa felt this the most, but they had felt compelled to obey the order, even though no sign of disease, poison, or radiation had been detected since the deadly tragedy.

Ralston considered all his options. He had too few. He might stay and work alone, but if he did so, Rasmussen might refuse to allow him to leave the planet with her researchers when Alpha Prime reached nova stage. The fear of alien disease still struck at the hearts of many otherwise sane people. Even though expert xenobiologists had shown it was impossible for an alien virus or bacterium not based on DNA to do any real damage to a human, primitive fears still persisted. And those races that shared DNA with mankind had produced no disease that didn't have an already existing—and known—counterpart. The human body was an ecology of living flora, microbes, and viruses. If an alien invader somehow found a niche and began growing, the body provided a natural defense to check it.

"Even though I wish there were a way of staying, I'll return with the rest of you, I suppose," he said. "The University will want to know firsthand the details of de la Cruz's death." Ralston laughed mirthlessly. "What I'll be able to tell them isn't going to be very enlightening, though."

"There hasn't been any hint of an answer in the dioramas?" Leonore asked.

"No, and you're to stay away from them. Understand me? That is a direct order."

"You're not being affected. The constant med monitoring shows you within norms." Leonore looked at her professor carefully. "But the last few readings have shown increased stress levels."

"Really?" Ralston said sarcastically. "The find of all time lies under my feet, a student dies exploring it, and the damned star will go nova before I can do more than photograph lifeless figures. Stress? Whatever might cause stress?"

"Michael, please. You know what I mean. You're taking this all on yourself."

"I'm in charge. The excavations in the city have shown nothing we haven't already guessed." He stared at the dewar with de la Cruz's body and then past it to the direction of the copper door leading to fame and something even headier: knowledge.

"The answer is down there. I know it. And I won't have time to find it!"

Frustration boiled over. Ralston stalked from the shelter just as the com unit beeped for his attention. He almost didn't return to answer. Let Leonore talk to Justine Rasmussen. But duty drew him just as Leonore reached for the signal button.

"I'll take it. Thanks."

"Dr. Ralston?" came the physicist's voice. "You still there?"

"Yes, Dr. Rasmussen, I'm still here. The alien slime monsters haven't devoured me yet."

"Your ship just shifted in. It'll be in orbit the day after tomorrow, E.T.A. noon."

He silently cursed. The damned pilot had come in exactly on target. A small error of just a microsecond of arc would have given an extra few days' intra-system travel. And even worse, the starship would enter orbit at precisely the best time for transfer. The pilot wasted not a single nanosecond.

"When will you leave?" asked Ralston.

"Our ship starred a few days after yours," she answered. "We'll stay as long as possible, but there's some discussion among my staff members about when that might be. The space-time tensors become distorted near a nova, and no one's sure what this might mean to the starship's engines."

Ralston didn't pretend to understand their concern, but it afforded him a chance. He mustered his courage, then almost blurted, "Could I stay behind and work, then leave with your group? I'm sure you'd have enough room aboard."

"I don't think that would be wise, Dr. Ralston," came Justine Rasmussen's cold voice. "There is still concern among my colleagues concerning the Pandora's box you seem to have opened."

"But—"

"Two days, Dr. Ralston. Be ready. The pilot told us he is anxious to return to Novo Terra as quickly as possible. And the University administration will want to discuss your student's death in some detail, I'm sure."

"Thank you." Ralston disconsolately flipped off the com unit. The absence of Rasmussen's voice and the static surrounding it made Ralston feel as if he'd stepped into a vacuum.

"There it is!" Asan cried with genuine animation. He pointed into Muckup's unusually clear sky at the bright silver spot. The starship had come for them.

"Is everything packed and ready?" Ralston asked needlessly. Since receiving Rasmussen's message two days ago, the entire camp had been ready for instant departure. Ralston had only haphazardly supervised, letting each student attend to his own belongings. The shelters and most of the equipment would be left. All Ralston personally packed were a few hardcopy photos and the analyzer block circuits that had recorded what had happened within the alien dioramas.

"It's not the end of the world," Leonore comforted.

Ralston laughed harshly. "It is. For Muckup. He looked around at the muddy plains and scraggly, off-green trees that reminded him of Earthly bonsai with their stunted height and contorted limbs. The biome had been devastated by the incessant rains, changing the face of the planet into not-quite-sea, not-quite-prairie. Whatever had caused the avian society's demise ten thousand years ago had also altered the weather patterns. His time spent in those few dioramas convinced him of that. Not a single scene showed the towering black thunderheads, the intense lightning storms, the incessant rain that had threatened to drive them all crazy.

"I'm sorry, Michael," Leonore said softly.

"About what?"

"Everything, I guess. Most of all about the dioramas."

They had attempted dismantling one to ship back to Novo Terra. While the figures moved easily enough, Ralston had been unable to preserve the telepathic messages after repositioning. Search as he might, he'd found no transmitter or other instrument projecting the thought lessons. Though he would bring back one figure, he could not transport the essence of the dioramas.

"We've got the photos and all the data from the analyzer. I can testify to the dioramas' effect. We recorded everything I said after leaving."

Leonore said nothing. They both knew that this meant little. Without analyzer readings to substantiate the claim of telepathic transfer, Ralston might have been inventing everything learned within the dioramas.

"It's not the end of my career," Ralston said. "But there's no future for me at the University of Ilium. After the hearings on de la Cruz's death, I'll be marked as a real pariah there. Every request for tenure will be disregarded." He shook his head. "That's nothing new, though. But even dead-end digs like Alpha 3 will be denied me. I'll end up like poor Pieter Nordon, doing nothing but classroom work, trapped in pointless lectures. Academe is the only place I know where they retire you to the primary business of the University."

Leonore said nothing. Research counted the most in the archaeology department—in any research-oriented department. Without the field trips, without choice selections for digs, a professor's career came to a slow halt. The department put those they wished to punish into the classroom to take the teaching burden off those on their way up in the hierarchy.

Fame and prominence came not from being a good professor but from being a good field researcher.

Michael Ralston's career was over, and they both knew it.

"A flare," called out Lantalman. "The pod's jets!"

Ralston squinted into the sun and saw the long orange flame from the transfer pod's engine. With an uncanny knack, the pilot landed almost precisely on the spot best suited for it. A solid rock foundation supported the landing gear; a dozen meters in any direction would have placed the pod on muddier, less stable ground.

Ralston ought to have counted this as a good sign. All he could think of was abandoning the find.

They trudged stolidly toward the grounded shuttle pod. Already the pilot and two crewmen swung out a loading crane. Contrary to Ralston's wishes, the first platform up contained the students' belongings. The second carried the eager students. Only then did Ralston convince the pilot to retrieve the dewar holding Yago de la Cruz's cryogenically frozen body.

"So you got him iced down, huh, Doc?" asked the pilot. He wrinkled his nose in distaste at the sight. "Damnedest thing I ever saw. How'd you come to think of it?"

"During the Nex-P'torra war the Nex preserved their wounded this way. They'd quick-freeze by dipping into liquid nitrogen, then thaw them out when they returned to a hospital."

The pilot fell silent. Ralston knew the starman had heard rumors of the crazy professor fighting for the Nex. Mention of the aliens' medical procedures had brought back the faint memories in the pilot and put them foremost in his mind. For Ralston's part, he was content not to bandy words with the pilot.

All he wanted was an end to this. To be off planet. To be away from Muckup. To be back on Novo Terra and hunting for a new position. He felt as if his life had come to an ignominious end.

And all because of Yago de la Cruz's greed in wanting to steal the find.

Ralston grunted when the pilot kicked in the jets and sent them skyward. Four hours later they docked with the starship. Seven hours after that, they starred for Novo Terra.

* * *

Michael Ralston walked under clear blue skies caught in the middle of a seasonably warm summer. While a heavier gravity than the one he had grown used to on Alpha 3 tugged at him, he didn't mind. Any gravity, great or small, was preferable to the weightlessness of star travel. He looked around the University campus and smiled. Students walked rapidly to and from classes, usually in small groups passionately arguing or quietly gossiping. A few lay beneath the trees or under the warm sun, catching up on needed sleep.

But the energy of the school transmitted itself to him. Ralston came more alive, renewed and eager. These students wanted to learn what he had to teach. They . . . they weren't his students, he corrected mentally. Not a single one was. The University Committee on Academics had relieved him of all duties— and pay—pending their investigation into de la Cruz's death.

Ralston stopped and stared at the green-domed building holding the committee offices. Few people entered and left this structure. Even fewer had business with the U.C.A. The classrooms were crowded, the student building overflowed onto the grounds, but the committee offices stayed virtually empty. Here decisions affecting a professor's academic life were made.

No one treaded those hallways lightly. Not when the slightest misstep produced a blighted future.

One or two of the passing students recognized him, but they quickly averted their eyes and walked faster. Ralston tried to blame them but couldn't. Who knowingly associates with a damned sinner summoned by the Inquisition?

His steps came slower now as he neared the building. He stared up at the green dome glistening in the sunlight. It ought to have been a beacon of hope. This was, after all, part of the University, an institution devoted to the pursuit of knowledge. All Ralston could picture was that dome falling to trap him. Beneath it he'd slowly suffocate, trapped like a bug in a bell jar, lost forever.

He looked for ways to avoid entering. To one side stood a news kiosk. He wandered over and saw that it had been tuned to the University station. The newsers were all students learning their trade.

Ralston shook his head. They didn't report news, not like their forerunners on Earth. He had studied how propaganda is written and recognized nothing but loaded phrases, subtle body movements, and clever distortions in the students' vidnewscast. A written text of their broadcast would reveal nothing but objective reporting.

As he watched, one slowly shook his head to indicate disapproval. So much for objectivity. But Ralston knew they trained for a hard market that had little to do with unbiased reporting. The newsers had become vid stars, actors editorializing.

"Bonita stuff, don't you agree?" came a voice so slick it must have been oiled.

It took Ralston a few seconds to recognize the woman as one of the newsers.

"Murra Tranton," she said, supplying the name that eluded Ralston.

"I've seen you on the vid kiosk," he said in as neutral a tone as possible. He knew what he faced inside this building—and what Murra Tranton wanted.

"Any comments, Dr. Ralston?" The woman's expression had been carefully rehearsed, he thought. She looked intelligent and concerned, interested and ready to aid him however she could.

He also thought she looked like a predatory beast, and no amount of acting could disguise that avarice.

He started to speak, then saw the vid pickup on her lapel. Anything he said would be transmitted back to the campus studio. Once there, he had no idea what they'd do with his words. Edit? Definitely. Change the question to any answer he might give? Possibly. Make him look like a bloody-handed butcher? If it served Murra Tranton's purpose. A story like this might get her recognized by the larger vidnews organizations.

Making a noncommittal gesture and saying nothing, he pushed past the newser. How had he gotten himself into such straits? It hardly seemed fair.

Ralston shook off the self-pity and went inside. The long marble halls were lined with wood-paneled doors. At precisely the hour when the cathedral clock chimed four, he entered the second door on the right without knocking. The inquisitors had gathered. Ralston looked around, expecting to see a black-hooded man standing beside a medieval Earth torture rack.

"Sit down, Dr. Ralston." The chairman of the U.C.A. pointed to a solitary seat in the center of the room. They isolated him as if he carried a virulent plague.

He sat.

"We have studied your report. Frankly, Doctor, we find it incomplete in all respects."

"Dr. Salazar, there wasn't adequate time to finish a report."

"You had a little over six weeks while starring back," another of the committee said. "Isn't that time enough?"

"The matter is complex," said Ralston, knowing they wouldn't listen to anything he said. They needed a scapegoat for de la Cruz's death. Since he'd been on the scene, he'd been elected already. "The alien museum with its dioramas is unique. Nothing like it has been—"

"Doctor," cut in Salazar, distaste altering his face into a mask of evil. Ralston tried to shake off that satanic image and found he couldn't. "We aren't here to discuss archaeology. Citizen de la Cruz's death is the only topic to be considered."

"But they tie together. I am sure that de la Cruz, by entering the dioramas without authorization or adequate precaution, triggered a telepathic projector and—"

"You're saying that Citizen de la Cruz caused his own demise? There's no evidence to support that, Dr. Ralston. You have produced not one shred of evidence for the existence of this so-called telepathic projector. No mechanism, no recording, nothing."

"As stated in the report, sir, the analyzer failed to detect it because I believe it is strictly a communication between biological entities."

"The last native of Alpha 3 died ten thousand years ago. No evidence has been given to show they still survive."

"The dioramas are unique," Ralston repeated. "And unknown. Their functioning is a mystery. I didn't have enough time to—"

"We're getting off the subject of Citizen de la Cruz's untimely death," interrupted Salazar. "Two of our late student's family have consented to appear today. Arturo and Constance de la Cruz, brother and sister of the deceased."

Ralston sat upright. He had been prohibited from speaking with any of de la Cruz's family. Now the committee brought two of them forward? For what purpose?

"He is the one?" came a voice from behind Ralston. He turned to see a man younger than Yago de la Cruz behind the chair. The family resemblance was obvious. Arturo de la Cruz shared his brother's insufferable arrogance.

"Citizens de la Cruz, thank you for coming," said Dr. Salazar.

"He even looks like a murderer," said Constance de la Cruz.

"Dr. Salazar, I protest!" Ralston shot to his feet. "This was supposed to be a closed hearing. Detailed minutes are being taken. I demand that Citizen de la Cruz's slanderous comment be deleted. I did *not* kill her brother nor did I allow him to die through any fault on my part."

"Liar," hissed the woman.

"Dr. Ralston, your protest is noted, but it is out of order. We are not assembled today to pass judgment. Rather, we gather information to decide whether to convene full hearings on this matter. Since we only investigate, the usual rules for conduct are suspended." Salazar made a brushing motion in Ralston's direction. "Do sit down and hold your tongue until you're addressed, Doctor."

"We will sue the University," promised Arturo de la Cruz. "My family will not rest until justice is served."

Ralston ignored Salazar's order and faced Yago de la Cruz's brother and sister. "I feel very deeply saddened by your brother's death. It is a fact, however, that field work is dangerous. Yago died advancing our knowledge of a newly discovered race with unknown powers. I did all I could to save him when the seizure struck. The automedic records will bear this out."

"You stole his discovery. The block circuits bear *that* out," shot back Arturo de la Cruz. "You killed him to take the discovery for yourself. That is apparent!"

"Citizens, please," called out Salazar. "We have gone over the records submitted by Dr. Ralston, we have conferred with medical authorities who are still conducting their autopsy of Citizen de la Cruz's body, and we have discussed the matter with University attorneys. In one week, formal hearings will be convened to decide on what actions, if any, should be taken in this matter. Until then, please accept the University of Ilium's condolences on the death of your brother."

The two de la Cruzes left without another word, both visibly furious and doing nothing to conceal it. Ralston simply sat in the chair and stared. Salazar hadn't addressed the decision to him—it had been for the de la Cruzes' benefit. The formal hearing would be a farce—any evidence he might present would be disallowed or ignored.

He had already been judged and found guilty.

Ralston didn't know which was worse, being placed in disgrace by his peers and possibly accused of murder, or losing the Alpha 3 dioramas for all time.

Without a word, Dr. Michael Ralston rose and marched from the room. The summer day outside the building no longer seemed so warm and cheerful.

TEN

"I'M NOT GOING to let them do this to me!" Michael Ralston raged. He paced back and forth in his tiny cubicle office and felt like bouncing from the walls. Caged. They had caged him like an animal, and he didn't like it.

"Really, Michael, it might not be that bad," Leonore Disa said without any conviction.

"Why hadn't you told me you'd turned down a chance to go with Velasquez to Proteus?" he asked, stopping to stare at her. She pushed a strand of brunette hair back to reveal the flashing plates on her forehead. They winked in soft pastel, Leonore's favorite, Ralston decided.

"It had no bearing on going to Alpha 3," she said simply.

"You wanted to be with Nels Bernssen."

"I'd be lying if I denied that. I love him."

"Does he love you?"

"That's none of your business." She sighed and folded her hands chastely in her lap. "In his way he does. He's so wrapped up in his project right now. No one's ever been this close to a pre-nova star. It'll make his career."

105

"The sort of discovery that wins awards," muttered Ralston, remembering his own find on Muckup. Muckup? Mucked up came closer to the truth. He cursed what seemed to be a cosmic balance. Bernssen had found his accolades in Alpha Prime's instability. That very same instability ruined Ralston's chances for a find equally as important.

"He's very good, Nels is."

"Who else at the University knows about his project? Someone I could talk to about novas. I always avoided the heavier science courses during my student years. All I cared about were archaeology and a bit of anthropology."

"Michael, please. The committee has suspended you until the hearing."

"They're going to flay me alive at the hearing," he said with some bitterness. "This is their chance to get rid of the professor who didn't kiss enough ass, who valued knowledge over politics. And they can do it ever so neatly. The de la Cruzes will ask for my head, and the University will give it to them. Simple."

"There's no way you could have prevented Yago's death."

"What's truth got to do with it?" Self-pity flooded him again, then burned away with a flame of determination. "Muckup's *my* discovery. I'm not going to let it go up in a flash of superheated plasma." He ignored his graduate student totally now, as if Leonore didn't even exist. "I can get back to Alpha 3. It won't be easy but I can do it. With a bit of additional, sophisticated equipment—most of what I'll need was left there —I can get enough for a paper. Automation. A supervisor-controller would be useful."

"But that's for controlling major robotic equipment," Leonore said, her head tipped to one side as she studied him.

"I can't ask anyone to risk their lives for this. I'll have to automate as much as I can."

"I can get a supervisor," Leonore said.

"How much?" he snapped, gray eyes sharp and hard.

"For free. My father owns Interstellar Computronics."

Ralston sank to the edge of his desk and simply stared. IC was one of the largest suppliers of automated equipment on Novo Terra. Leonore came from a family so wealthy that Ralston couldn't even guess within an order of magnitude what their worth must be.

"You'd do that for me?"

"No one else around here seems to recognize the importance of this find. I do."

"I can arrange to star back in a week."

"How? Not on any of the University starships."

Ralston smiled. "I've still got contacts. Don't worry about that. You *can* get a supervisor?"

Leonore nodded. "What else would you need? I'm afraid Daddy's company doesn't manufacture much else in the way of robotic research equipment."

"I can get the rest. Most of it," he amended. Ralston's enthusiasm died a little when logic reclaimed him. He looked at Leonore suspiciously and asked, "What do you want in return for this? Your name's already on the paper as co-author. You know that."

"I don't have nearly enough data to do an adequate dissertation," she said, not angry that he accused her of motives other than altruism. "I want to go back with you."

"No Leonore, no supervisor?"

"That's putting it so harshly, Dr. Ralston," Leonore said.

"But it's accurate." Ralston frowned, then let a smile dawn. "I don't care if it's the diorama find or Nels Bernssen that's drawing you back to Muckup. When we're finished with that planet, we'll both be famous."

"I'll be content with a good thesis," she said. Leonore rose and left Ralston's office.

Ralston sat and stared out a tiny window across the Quad. A statue of Bacon gleamed in Novo Terra's warm sunlight. Even though Ralston couldn't read the inscription from this distance, he knew it by heart: "For knowledge, too, is itself a power."

"Verd, I know Nels Bernssen," the research assistant said. He looked up from the terminal where he'd scattered papers and block readers. "Good instincts. And a damn fine mathematician. Wish I had his skill there. Might have done better on my comps. But you're not here to offer me some tutoring, are you? What can I do for you, Dr. Ralston?"

Ralston glanced at the nameplate above the terminal. "You're Liu Chen?"

"Chen Liu, but don't worry about getting my name wrong.

Even the University computer gets confused. Call me Chen."

Ralston pulled a chair up and leaned on Chen's small, cluttered desk, his elbows resting on a thick mat of paper covered with intricate doodlings.

"Here, let me take some of that," Chen said, obviously distraught over Ralston's disturbing the order of his mess. "Not too many use paper for their calculations. Never could get the feel of looking at it on a screen."

"I need some information about novas."

"Since Nels is off on Alpha 3, damn his bones, you've come to the right place. Simply put, a nova is a star that goes *bang!*"

"You don't like Nels?"

"I *love* the man. And I envy him. Being right up there to witness the early stages. While my interests lie more in what happens after the bang, I'd still like to be there nudging Nels' elbow, getting him to take readings on parameters that count."

"What makes Alpha Prime so unusual? I don't know much about the H-R star classes but I gather it's the wrong type to go nova."

"Verd," Chen agreed. "Take a look at my big project." He punched in a few long code words. A nebula leaped into focus on the screen. "I've sent a couple probes to the 1054 'guest star' to study the accretion disk."

"The gaseous disk around it?"

Chen looked at Ralston, then nodded. "We call it the 1054 because that's when it was seen on Earth. They call it the Crab Nebula, but it doesn't look like one from here." He brightened even more. "In China it was well documented. They called any nova a 'guest star' because it grew brighter and brighter, then faded away. A guest.

"My work is coming to a chinging dead end and I don't know why." Chen thumped a pile of papers to one side of his terminal. "My first automated probe just broke down."

"No more telemetry?"

Chen nodded glumly. "Can't figure out what went wrong, either. The best I can determine from the readings I got, some flaw in the block circuitry caused the failure."

"That's a bit unusual, isn't it?"

"Verd," Chen agreed. "We always check those babies out to a zillionth of a decimal place. Cost too damn much to have them go wrong five hundred light years from the nearest screwdriver. But random electronics failures *do* happen. But why to me?"

"Your other probe's still sending back information, isn't it?"

"I guess so." Chen turned even gloomier. "The data I expected aren't showing up. Nothing matches. Some of it is so far off beam I'm beginning to think that I'm looking at a second electronics failure. Won't be able to get the University to spring for any more probes, either. Too chinging expensive. When everything's getting confusing and we have a chance to learn something really deep, they cut off our funding."

Chen shook his head and stared at the star field on his screen.

"But Alpha," urged Ralston. "Is it interesting because you can put observers close by?"

"That's part of it. The rest is as perplexing on the good side as my probe failures are on the bad. Alpha is the wrong spectral type. It's a G5, not a B7 like my 'guest star.'" Chen shook his head. "Do envy Nels, that son of a bitch. A real chance to shake up all our theories about stellar evolution. The spectrographic readings alone are worth a dozen papers. Nels is seeing iron sublimations in the photosphere. Hope he loosens up and shares some of it with me. I can do a lot for him after the primary goes." Chen's face lit like the nova he discussed. "There's got to be an accretion disk. I can watch it forming. Be a novel idea to co-author with him. The dynamic instability leading to formation of accretion."

"Do you have any idea how long before Muckup—Alpha 3—becomes dangerous?"

"Dangerous now," Chen said. "Oh, you mean how long before the radiation from the primary fries everything on the planet?" He shook his head. "No way of telling. There'll be an initial intense burst of x-rays, if our theories are accurate, followed by a powerful solar wind composed mostly of highly energetic protons. Heavy ionizing radiation," he said, more to himself than to Ralston. "Then?" Chen shrugged.

"The planet is vaporized?"

"Verd. But the timetable for it is murky. We just can't predict to the nanosecond. I'd say that it's less than six months away."

"No more?"

"Might be less. A lot less."

Ralston left. At first he walked with shoulders bowed. Then he began to straighten. Resolve hardened within him. There could be no hesitation, he realized. To vacillate now meant lost opportunity. The civilization on Alpha 3 must not die unexamined.

And it wouldn't. Even if Michael Ralston had to die along with the planet.

"I can't do it, Doc. No way I can get a chinging starship on such short notice." The man looked around nervously, as if expecting police to arrest him. "You sure it's safe here?"

"The Quad's as safe as any place I know," Ralston told him. "I didn't want to risk my office."

"Got it eared?"

Ralston solemnly nodded, playing the paranoid game. "There's no way to know who might be listening," he agreed. "Out here, there's open spaces and enough noise and people going by to cover whatever we say."

"They got good circuits. They can pick up a feather dropping in the middle of a rocket test. Hell, the student newsers got snoops able to do better'n that."

"That's why we've got to keep moving. We dare not let them catch up." Ralston wondered who the man feared—or if anyone truly sought him. He had seen others like this man after the war. They had turned inward, examining themselves and finding only a hollow shell. To give meaning to their emptiness they had fantasized cabals and plots and persecution.

Ralston knew the man needed psychologic aid, but he couldn't bring himself to suggest it, not with the radical chemical and electronic techniques used by those in the field.

"Cost you a chinging fortune, Doc. You know it."

"I can pay. For the cause," he added, almost as an afterthought. This sealed the deal.

"Two days. Take a shuttle pod up and follow the beacon. Two whites and a red. No other contact."

The man slipped away, mingled in the crowd of students watching a news kiosk, and vanished as if he'd never existed. Ralston sat under a large cryptomeria, his back against the rough bark. In a way, the man he'd just dealt with didn't exist. At least, not officially. Somehow, he had managed to expunge his name from all computer records. Ralston had never heard a name mentioned, nor did he ask. That would violate a trust.

He briefly considered a life at the fringes of society, providing contraband, smuggling, shipping that which no one else dared ship. Ralston laughed ruefully. That wasn't the kind of life he wanted for himself. The University of Ilium stretched out in front of him, living greens mingling with artificial browns, the soft scents of summer wrinkling his nose, students hurrying to classes, discussing their lives and newfound knowledge, a tranquil oasis of learning.

For all the students who only put in their time, he knew there were others who sought to learn, really learn. For those cherished students, he'd gladly devote his life.

Ralston found himself missing the classroom work, the fostering of education. Sometimes he felt like pounding heads to get an idea into an especially dense skull, but the rewards, for the most part, were worth the effort. The sight of a face brightening as a concept penetrated, the student who clearly stood out as exceptional, the rush of new knowledge, new discoveries, new methods of work.

He lived for this. The University sheltered Ralston from the pressures that drove the man he'd just spoken with past the bounds of accepted behavior. In return, Ralston performed the generally pleasurable chore of educating students. And writing his research papers.

All this was worth fighting for. Ralston wouldn't lightly surrender it because of the unfortunate accident that had taken Yago de la Cruz's life.

"We triumph without glory when we triumph without danger," he said softly. "Knowledge is dangerous to gain and dangerous to use. But we need it. Oh, yes, how we need it. How *I* need it." Ralston couldn't conceive of an existence without progress, without the promise of new and wondrous revelations and the chance to explore them fully.

A chanting from across the Quadrangle disturbed his thoughts. He leaned over and peered past the statue of Bacon in the center. A tight knot of students—not more than thirty—shouted something he didn't hear clearly and thrust their fists at the azure sky.

Such vehemence surprised Ralston. He didn't think he'd been away from the University so long that he had missed out on the formation of new campus action groups. Apparently, he had.

Ralston plucked a blade of grass and sucked at the juices,

trying to channel his thoughts to Muckup and the equipment he needed. It was nothing short of a miracle that Leonore Disa could supply the supervisor. That would insure a dozen times more work being done than he might achieve alone.

He frowned when he thought of her demand to be allowed to accompany him. While Ralston hated to deceive her, he couldn't allow her to return with him to Alpha 3. The danger outweighed keeping his word. All he had to do was drop a word to his mysterious friend that Leonore was one of "them" and she'd be led astray.

In two days he'd be aboard the starship bound for Alpha 3—and she'd be in the middle of the Quad staring up at the empty sky.

The chanting again disturbed his concentration. The students had begun moving toward the statue. Ralston went cold inside when he heard their chants.

"Kill the Nex-lover!" the small crowd roared.

Michael Ralston had no trouble deciding they meant him. No one else in the University fit that description so well.

One student climbed onto Bacon's statue and held on to the precarious perch with one hand. The other waved vigorously to emphasize his obviously popular words.

"He is a menace! We cannot allow such warmongers and traitors to exist among us. Bigotry must be cut out and destroyed to make a better society!"

"And he killed Yago!" came the bull-throated cry from the crowd. The others picked up on de la Cruz's first name. "Yago, Yago, Yago!" the crowd chanted.

"For that alone Ralston should be barred from the University."

Raucous shouts of agreement and encouragement rose from the growing crowd. Ralston didn't stir. Movement might attract unwanted attention. He looked over those assembled, trying to find students he recognized. Sometimes, students disgruntled with low grades formed into such groups to take out their frustrations. He saw no one who'd ever been in any of his classes.

What he did see angered him. A gray-skinned, thick-fleshed P'torra stood to one side as an observer rather than as an active participant. Short, bulbous fingers worked at the tiny keyboard of a hand-held electronic device. Ralston had often seen the

P'torra use these "impulse drivers" to devastating advantage. A P'torra entered human psychological parameters and, with the intensity of responses to key words from whoever harangued the crowd, got out a detailed blueprint of how to more effectively manipulate behavior.

The P'torra signaled to his human co-conspirator, who shifted from the bigotry theme to one of praise for Yago de la Cruz. The crowd's reaction mounted exponentially. They had been angry before. Now they reached a peak where murder wasn't inconceivable.

The P'torra's blubbery lips pulled back to reveal twin rows of needle-sharp teeth. He had found the crowd's resonance frequency with this topic. His impulse driver had again proven its worth in controlling human behavior.

Ralston slowly rose, the tree guarding his back. He slowly circled the tree and placed it between him and the crowd. He walked quickly toward his office, trying not to draw attention.

He failed.

Ralston heard the impassioned cries go up from the crowd as the man haranguing from the statue sighted him. Decorum dictated that he not change his pace. Common sense told him he'd be torn apart if the crowd caught him on the Quad. Ralston ran as if all the demons of hell nipped at his heels.

And, as far as he was concerned, at least one did: the P'torra.

A large rock whirled past his head and smashed into the office building. He ducked and got through the door. Another rock crashed against the clear plastic pane. Ralston vainly sought some way of locking the door. A magnetic key was required; only the night patrol was likely to have one properly coded.

Ralston thought about barring himself in his office, then discarded the idea as suicidal. If the crowd trapped him there, they could do any number of things. While most University buildings were relatively fireproof, papers still burned and plastics melted. The fumes from the plastic might not be deadly, but they'd certainly be dangerous if the crowd held him prisoner within his office.

He hurried toward the far end of the building. An exit there would allow him to slip out the back way and elude the crowd. Sooner or later, even the lethargic campus security squad would arrive to contain the students.

Ralston skidded to a halt. "Damn!" Somehow they had

already circled the building and cut off his escape. "The P'torra plotted this out. He had to!" Crowds did not operate with such foresight. Ralston saw no other explanation for the students' coordinated efforts to capture him.

He ducked through a door leading into the cellar. Ralston slammed it behind him and leaned against it, heart pounding. He slowly regained his breath. In the corridor he heard the harsh footsteps of a dozen or more pursuers.

"Where'd he go? Where did that chinging son of a bitch go?"

"Check the offices!" another shouted.

"Coolness," came a soft voice. "Composure. Examine the lower reaches of this edifice."

The P'torra!

Ralston ran down the stairs, new knowledge bursting on him in that instant.

He knew how a trapped rat felt.

The door opened and the students rushed after him.

ELEVEN

"KILL HIM!"

The echoes reverberated down the long hallway and through the dusty crates stored in the cellar. The sound of pursuit gave Michael Ralston the added speed he needed to find a small storage room, slip inside, then close the door and block it the best he could.

He stared in horror at the tiny box he'd shoved in front of the door. It wouldn't hold back a crowd spurred on by the P'torra's psychological needlings. It'd hardly hold back a stiff breeze. Ralston's fear rose, then slowly faded as reason regained a hold. If he acted like a hunted animal, that was the way he'd die.

Only thinking this through afforded him any hope for escape. Forcing himself to breathe deeply, he calmed more and more. He closed his eyes and found the Nex-embedded hypnotic commands deep within. They hadn't understood how humans entered battles keyed and nervous. A few deft lessons with their combat psychologists had given Ralston the control needed to keep an edge but not be pushed into panic.

He shook his head. He had tried to deny that training because of the war and the way his peers reacted to the Nex. No more. He needed every advantage possible if he wanted to get away from the mob and leave Novo Terra for Alpha 3.

Gray eyes darted around the small storage room, checking, evaluating, hypothesizing, discarding. The window out of the room was far too small for him to squeeze through—and freedom tantalized him on the other side. The bright blue sky shone with the glow of a new lover, and Novo Terra's summer winds promised life eternal.

Ralston pulled a crate under the window and jumped atop its sagging wood surface. A desperate jerk tore the window's lock from the wall. He flung it open so hard that the plastic window popped out of its frame and clattered to the floor. Ralston jumped and cut both arms on the sides of the window. With trembling fingers, he pulled threads from his shirt and stuck them onto the frame. Only then did he jump to one side and crawl into an empty box barely large enough to contain him. He pulled his makeshift blind in close, leaving only a crack through which to peer into the room.

Barely had he hidden when the door burst inward. A rush of confused colors passed his narrow cone of vision. At least five students had entered the room.

Ralston's nose wrinkled. The P'torra with his distinctive body odor had also entered.

"He got away!" cried one of the men.

"A moment," came the P'torra's sharp command. Ralston heard the crate on which he'd stood creak under the alien's ponderous weight. He imagined the P'torra running a stubby finger along the window frame, finding the blood, bringing it to his slit-nostriled nose, then lightly sampling it with the tip of his tongue. Then the P'torra would bend closer, check the fibers. The alien's mind would make odd leaps of intuition not shared by humans.

"In this, you find surety. He got away," the P'torra announced, finally convinced. "Please to seek him out. Dr. Ralston is a danger to all spirited beings."

Footsteps shuffled from the room. Ralston waited. He knew the P'torra mind—and his nose still wrinkled. After long minutes, Ralston heard a slight creaking sound. The alien shifted position on the crate on which he sat. Ralston's mind raced. If he emerged to confront the P'torra, he knew he could physically overpower the alien. He had met enough in single combat to learn their weaknesses. For all their bulk and muscle, they moved slowly to achieve certain positions. He might lure the P'torra to bend slightly from the waist; this constrained motion around their hips. A quick turn to the side, a blow to the side of the neck, death.

Ralston pictured it all clearly in his mind.

But he waited. After another five minutes, the creaking noises sounded once more, this time accompanied by soft footsteps. What had the P'torra thought about while he waited? The same things that Ralston had? Vulnerability and advantage? Or something so totally bizarre no human could share it?

Ralston waited a few more minutes, then slowly pushed aside the box and peered into the room. Warm afternoon sunlight slanted through the destroyed window. Ralston straightened stiffened joints and cautiously looked out into the cellar's central corridor. Empty. He jumped atop the crate again and looked out across a grassy area leading down to the University's athletic fields. In the distance he saw the cathedral's tall central spire and heard the chimes sounding the hour.

"Now they come," he grumbled when he saw six uniformed men trotting along the walkways. The University security police had arrived to disperse the crowd. More than a hundred students protested. As he watched, the security force used sleep gas against the more violent protestors, but Ralston knew that the P'torra wouldn't be among them. Always the alien would hold back, stay at the periphery, incite but never participate. That was the P'torra way.

Ralston retraced his path through the cellar and back up to the ground level. He considered going to his second-floor office, then discarded the notion. If the P'torra really wanted his blood, students would be posted there to alert the mob. Ralston walked briskly down the hall, found the westernmost door and left through an arboretum. The overhanging limbs of the trees and large shrubs gave him a sense of security. Away from prying eyes and masked by the cloying floral perfumes from the nose slits of the P'torra, Ralston walked aimlessly until he circled around to face the athletic fields.

The crowd had vanished. The security force no doubt breathed

a sigh of relief at their day's work. And this brief interruption
of the University's tranquillity had passed. Ralston went to one
of the outlying buildings and slipped inside, taking care not to
be seen. He found a shadowy corner in a balcony overlooking
the gymnasium floor. With a sigh, he sank into a chair and
once again forced himself to relax. The effort this time proved
more successful than before.

The danger had passed. Temporarily.

On the floor two teams played mag ball, shuttling a light,
metal-encased cork ball back and forth using electromagnetic
wands. Each side was allowed only so much charge. The mag
ball might be passed back and forth between team members a
dozen times or more, as long as each used only a fraction of
their allotted energy, or one player might use all the team's
charge in getting the mag ball over the net. If the ball touched
ground, a point was scored. As with most games, it required
skill and teamwork—and was a game Ralston never appreciated.

"Did you come to play or just ogle all the sweet young girls
strutting about in their shorts?"

Ralston whirled at the voice, banging his elbow against the
wall.

"My, aren't you the jumpy one? I've *got* to fence with you
today. I really do. This is my best chance in months and months
to win. You'll be a real sucker for even my lousy feints if you
keep overreacting like that, Michael."

"Sorry, Druanna," he said, settling back into the chair and
rubbing his elbow. "You startled me."

"Hiding out, eh?"

"Nothing gets by you, does it?" He stared at Druanna Thorkkin, wondering how much she knew and how much she'd only
guessed. The woman was sharp, he'd have to grant her that.
He sighed. She looked so much like another he'd known. The
same light brown hair falling in soft waves, the same flush to
the cheeks from being perpetually excited by life, the same
vitality and imagination and piercing intelligence.

So much like Marta.

Ralston had never gotten it clear in his own mind whether
he enjoyed Druanna's company because of the resemblance to
that love long lost, or if he actually appreciated her for herself.

"I was down in the office when the call came for the security force. Those fools came blundering back after they'd so valiantly defended the University's honor. The P'torra, wasn't it?"

Druanna Thorkkin didn't share his dislike of the blubbery aliens, nor did she much appreciate the reptilian aspect of the Nex. But she was a friend.

"I think so."

"You've really stirred up a fuss around here. Makes a staid old University like Ilium sit up and take notice. I think you're good for the creeping lethargy I see around here." Druanna looked at Ralston for a moment, then said, "You're not here for a match, are you?"

"No. Hiding out is closer to it."

"A pity. I could use a good workout. Foil? Saber? You sure?"

Ralston shook his head. Druanna Thorkkin was the only one at the University who shared his enthusiasm for fencing. The others considered it an anachronism, as they did his passion for other Earthly skills and pursuits. After the brief nuclear exchange, Earth had become little more than a backwater in human affairs. Novo Terra had assumed the role of leadership in political and economic matters, but Ralston still felt a kinship to the planet of his birth. Fencing was just one of the arts that he considered worthy of remembering.

"Grave-robbing isn't what it used to be," Druanna said sadly. "You used to be more alive. Just the hint of me besting you at foil sent you into a spiraling orbit."

"You're quicker than I am," he admitted, "but what makes you think I've given up the sport?"

"I can't taunt you into a match," she said. "Or is it more than stark, shuddering fear of being beaten that stays your mighty sword?" Druanna cocked her head to one side and peered at him. "The P'torra's not doing this? Are you afraid of Salazar?"

"Verd. I'm afraid of what Salazar and the committee will do to me."

"Green shit from a purple cow, Ralston! You're not even lying so's I believe you."

"I'd better be going."

"I think that's exactly what you're going to do," she said firmly. "You're going back to Alpha 3, aren't you? Without University sanction, unless I missed all the clues."

"You're speculating. I can't do anything until the hearing.

Maybe I can't do anything after it."

Druanna went on, as if she hadn't heard a word he said. "That funny man with no name you find so interesting. You know the one I mean. The one who's sure everyone's spying on him. He's got the connections to smuggle you back, doesn't he? You're going to star out to your dig. You left the equipment on Alpha 3, so to hell with the primary going nova. Is that it, Michael?"

"You've been reading those quaint mysteries I loaned you," Ralston said.

"The Doyles were good, but I liked the Blocks and Ulfbloms better. And I can read you just like I do them. Better, since I don't have to turn your pages."

Ralston stared at her. He liked Druanna for her wit and intelligence, but this time she pushed into territory he wanted left unexplored.

"You," she said, eyes narrowing and finger pointing, "are going to be in more trouble than you can handle if you go back."

"Do I have a choice?"

"I suppose not," Druanna said. "The find's that important, is it?"

Ralston smiled broadly. "Thank you. I appreciate it."

"What?"

"That you knew the only thing drawing me to Alpha 3 was the museum, that I wasn't running away from the hearing because of what happened to de la Cruz."

"Never occurred to me. I know you grave robbers. All wrapped up in your work like a mummy. If de la Cruz had been one of your graduate students instead of one who caught the consolation prize in the grades lottery, I'd've thought you worked him to death."

"It was accidental. I've been thinking about it. A lot. And some other things, too. Those I can't quite put into words, but the de la Cruz death is a part of it." Ralston leaned forward, looking at the mag ball players without really seeing them. "De la Cruz entered one of the last dioramas. Something happened there that killed him. Something that didn't show up in earlier scenes."

"You believe it might give a clue to the culture's decline?"

"It might not be the cause, but it has to be significant. I

experienced nothing but the telepathic communication in the first few dioramas."

"Handy gadget," mused Druanna. "I wish I could teach my students mind to mind. Those that have minds would benefit, and I'd find out quicker about the others."

"I'd like to get the mind projector, too," Ralston admitted. "The notes I found in de la Cruz's belongings showed he was interested only in the commercial exploitation of the gadget. But there's so much more, even if I can't bring away a working projector to tear apart and reverse engineer."

"The society?"

"Dead. And the decline came so quickly. Their capital city had been razed. It's as if the dioramas were their last real effort to pass along their history."

"You think the last ones show what happened and that de la Cruz died from it. Interesting conjecture."

Druanna Thorkkin leaned back and hiked her feet to the balcony guard rail. She laced strong fingers behind her head and looked at Ralston out of the corner of her eye.

"It's a mean job for anyone to help you find out what happened to de la Cruz—and the folks on Alpha 3."

"I don't want you to get involved."

"I didn't volunteer. I just pointed out what Salazar would say."

In silence they watched as the far team won the mag ball game. Sweaty, laughing students laid down their playing electrodes and left for the showers.

"I've got so much money I hardly know what to do with it," Druanna said.

"I can't take it."

"I didn't offer it. Just talking. Don't think Salazar would consider it collusion on my part, either, if some of that money just happened to vanish from my account and show up in yours. You're going to need a great deal, Michael."

"If that star goes nova, you may never see any of your money back."

"My loss is going to be bigger than a few months' wages lost," she said. "Hell, Michael, I'll have lost the only fool on this campus I can out-fence."

Ralston turned, reached out and laid his fingertips on the line of Druanna's jaw. He bent over, lightly kissed her on the lips, and said, "Thank you."

Druanna snorted and pulled away. "What's got into me, consorting with known grave robbers?" She rose and walked off, never looking back. Ralston sank into the chair and let his mind race ahead. He had so much to plan, so much to do.

But first he had to make one last visit. Ralston wasn't sure he wanted to see Westcott. Some people were just too strange for him to bear, and Westcott was one of them.

"Something Chen said bothered me," he told Westcott. Ralston stared at the mathematician and wondered if the man heard or not. Westcott had shaved his head to better accommodate the remote IR interface mounted there. Ralston shivered. No matter that Westcott had all the permits and authorizations required to connect himself directly into his beloved computers, the sight of a man with the flesh-mounted plugs and remote IR devices made him uneasy.

Ralston wasn't overly religious but he understood the Church's injunction against such meddling with the human spirit. It seemed sacrilegious.

Westcott leaned back, eyes hooded and a dreamy expression on his face. He reached up and made some minute adjustment to the infrared remote control device atop his head. He smiled, but Ralston shivered even more at it. The smile wasn't human.

"I'm so slow," Westcott murmured, almost a croon to put a baby to sleep. "So slow, but my loving friends, they're so fast, so wondrously fast."

Ralston looked away from the man, if Westcott could be called that. Even the Nex seemed more human than the mathematician. A single framed diploma decorated the walls of Westcott's laboratory. Ralston looked at it more closely. As he'd thought, this wasn't a diploma in the strictest sense. It was Westcott's license to direct-connect with a computer. Only a few ever applied and less than one in a thousand of those applying were granted what Ralston considered a dubious privilege.

Westcott spoke directly to his computer's block circuits, saw with the computer's laser probes, felt with piezoelectric plates, heard with amplifiers, smelled with surface acoustic wave sensors—what truly human function remained in the mathematician? Not emotions, of that Ralston was certain.

He wished that the planetary licensing authorities had totally outlawed such human-computer connection instead of severely restricting it.

From the contented expression on Westcott's hatchet-thin face, however, Ralston knew where to find one dissenting vote to his gut-level reaction.

"Not brilliant, but sound," Westcott said.

"What?"

"Chen. You mentioned Chen Liu. Or has it already been erased from your memory?"

"Something Chen said disturbed me."

"Emotion," cut in Westcott, "has no place in science."

"He mentioned a nova seen on Earth in 1054. He mentioned losing a robot probe, possibly two, that he'd recently started out to investigate the accretion disk."

"Interesting dynamics in the disk," whispered Westcott, eyes closed now. The light on his interface unit blinked a baleful red. Across the room, the IR beam impinged on a sensor plate and transferred Westcott's thoughts directly into the computer. Another IR unit broadcast back the computer's results.

"The Alpha primary is going nova."

"Much of interest mathematically," said Westcott. "The tensors for the region are showing..." His voice trailed off to nothing.

Ralston rushed on, wanting only to state his case, see if Westcott would help, and then get the hell out of the lab. "I know the 1054 'guest star' and Alpha Prime represent only two points and thus can be connected with a straight line—" Ralston waited for comment. None came. "I tried to extrapolate along that line to see if there were other novas occurring. I didn't find anything. But the *feel* is there. Something else ought to be found from this data."

"A straight line?" scoffed Westcott, showing that he had, indeed, been listening. "You naively assumed a linear trajectory?"

Westcott did nothing, but an entire wall screen glowed a pale blue. Tiny points began appearing. To Ralston's eye, they were randomly distributed. But then the display began to change, to turn, to give a new perspective. A dotted red line ran smoothly from one point to the next, forming a distinct nonlinear curve.

"This takes into account not only appropriate novas, but

also proper motion of the stars, drag from gas clouds and other variations in gravity wells."

Ralston stared at the dozen or so points. "What are they? All novas?"

"You asked for that, didn't you?" The scorn in Westcott's voice irritated Ralston. "Here is a different view of the same data. A time variable has been added."

This confused him. The points along the curve appeared at random—but all the points eventually showed on the graph. The point that interested him most eventually winked into being: Alpha 3 lay in the path. With the 1054 star the last point, and the Alpha primary two points in the past by ten thousand years, Ralston began getting a sense of inevitability to what he witnessed.

"Something following this trajectory might be causing the stars to go nova," he said. "But there seems to be a time delay from point to point. One star might go nova long before stars on either side along the trajectory."

Westcott sat as still as any granite statue. His gaunt face seemed to shrink and the red light indicating computer access blinked faster and faster until it shone constantly.

Ralston went to Westcott and placed a hand against the man's throat. The flesh felt dry and leathery; no pulse throbbed in the arteries. He moved his hand under Westcott's nose. The faintest of warm breath issued forth. Ralston jerked away when the red indicator light began to blink at a speed detectable by the human eye. When it flashed only once every second, Westcott opened his eyes.

"A problem of great interest." For the first time, Westcott's expression showed some humanity. "Curious that one of your type would stumble across this problem and have the intelligence to recognize it for what it is."

"Then something might follow that dotted line and be causing the suns to explode?"

"A high probability exists. That is not the question. Rather, how is this accomplished? The mathematics of chaos has not been properly examined for"—the red light flashed once on his interface—"since the twenty-first century on Earth. On Earth." Westcott snickered, as if this were the dirtiest joke he'd ever heard.

"What does this moving *thing* do?" asked Ralston.

"The mathematical intricacy of the problem is worthy of my time."

With that, Westcott closed his eyes. The interface indicator light began pulsating once more. Ralston stopped and considered running his hand through the IR beam connecting cortex with computer.

"Don't," came Westcott's warning. "It gives me a headache."

Ralston started, then forced calm on himself. It was as if a corpse had risen from the grave to speak. He quickly left Westcott's laboratory without breaking the IR remote sensor beam. Ralston wasn't certain what he'd learned, other than Alpha 3's civilization had died because of something that had passed by.

Now the star was going nova.

How did all this tie in with Yago de la Cruz's death and the dioramas? Ralston had to know.

TWELVE

MICHAEL RALSTON LEFT the mathematician's office feeling unclean. He had nothing against Westcott as a researcher; it was generally admitted that Westcott had few peers in the abstract geometries where he lived. Nor did Ralston fault Westcott for his undeniable dedication to his work. He shuddered involuntarily at the thought of being so closely tied to a computer. While Ralston depended heavily on their use in the field—and in the classroom—the concept of oneness with a machine troubled him deeply.

Ralston stopped at the door leading from the laboratory and quickly scanned the University's spacious grounds. The sylvan setting had always soothed him—it had been one of the reasons he had accepted the University's niggardly offer to teach archaeology. When the pressures of too many students, too much politics, too little time all came crushing in on him, Ralston had walked through the grounds and retreated to a better time.

For him, that time was more fantasy than reality. Earth had never been like this, even before the quick war. His earliest

childhood memories were of smog-filled skies, acid rains that
stung the skin and burned the eyes, snow that fell black with
soot, yellowish plumes of sulfur dioxide rising into the air, and
his father talking of radon gas from fossil fuel combustion
shortening their lives. The dinosaurs' revenge, his father had
always said with a cynical laugh.

Ralston didn't think of the Earth war as positive, but it
seemed only a faster version of death to him. Choke on noxious
fumes and glow blue from burning coal and heavy industry, or
go up in a swift radioactive cloud.

Slow or fast. He wasn't sure which was the better death.

But he didn't have that to worry about on Novo Terra. All
on-planet manufacturing had been banned soon after coloni-
zation two hundred years ago. What needed to be built was
done in orbit where the detritus of industry could be disposed
of safely. Most of the electricity on the planet came from
orbiting genosynchronous solar power stations. The high-
intensity beams to the ground afforded some leakage of microwave radiation, but it was a small price to pay for not
sucking in flyash with every breath. The surface of Novo Terra
had been transformed into a garden with strict laws to maintain
it.

Ralston inhaled deeply and caught the subtle fragrances
wafting on the gentle breeze. But when he closed his eyes he
saw only the mud flats of Muckup, the copper door and the
museum of death beneath Alpha 3's surface. Ralston screwed
his eyes shut all the tighter and winced at his mental image of
the planet vanishing in a sudden flare of a nova.

He knew such a sight would be impossible. The highest
speed framing cameras, or even electronic block cameras, would
be incapable of capturing the final instant of Alpha 3's life. If
such things were possible, a human observer would see only
a purple flash as the speed-of-light radiation burned out optic
nerves.

Even this was fantasy. The slowness of impulse transmission
along nerve paths would prevent any sight of the nova at all.
Ten thousand centimeters a second versus thirty billion centimeters a second. His body and brain wouldn't respond fast
enough to the stimulus, not by a factor of three million.

Ralston shook himself free of such morbid thoughts. He
cared nothing for the destruction of Alpha 3; he wanted its

preservation. More precisely, he wanted to preserve whatever might be uncovered about the populace that had lived on the planet. Knowledge of this magnitude should not be lost.

Even in Nature's fierce, cleansing nova fire.

Ralston looked around to Novo Terra's primary. The sun quietly slipped behind a row of greenery to the west and cast long, distorted shadows across the grounds. To think that Alpha 3's sun looked so much like this one. Ralston didn't want to think that whatever caused that nova might also be capable of triggering another.

The main room of the library stretched before him, virtually deserted for the evening meal. One or two librarians sat hunched over their glowing consoles, rearranging their databases for the hundredth time that month, seeking new ways of making searches more esoteric, thus protecting their jobs for another pay period. They knew that their positions were tolerated, long since unnecessary because of easy access to their information from any point on campus. But old traditions died hard, especially in academic circles.

Ralston tried to imagine a university without a library and failed. It might be an anachronism, but symbols usually were. He had never seen a promotional advertising for a school that didn't include at least one zoomshot of the library, a quiet spot for reflection and study, a quick and still meaningful representation of the entire higher educational system in one location.

He settled into one of the saddles and thumbed on the terminal. At the prompt, he typed in his departmental billing code number. Ralston frowned when it took a dozen seconds to respond. The authorization finally blinked on the screen.

His fingers flew over the keys, demanding information, ordering it sent to the hardcopy room, asking for more. In less than five minutes he had finished. Ralston looked over his right shoulder toward the door. No one. Over his left he saw a solitary librarian behind a desk digging out a sandwich for dinner.

The feeling of being watched had halted his work. And now that sensation forced him away from the console and toward the hardcopy room at a pace only slightly less than a run.

The imprinter had spat out a stack of plastic sheets for him. He was one of the few who bothered with hardcopy. Most had the information placed in their computer files or had it burned onto a block for viewing later. But as an archaeologist, Ralston lived for the past. Some even accused him of living *in* the past.

He pulled the sheets from the imprinter and began riffling through them, but his eyes weren't focused on the pages. His nose wrinkled from an unexpected odor. Hairs rose on the back of his neck, as if he'd touched a high-voltage electrode. He didn't have to turn to know who blocked his exit from the room.

"Did you bring your mob with you?" Ralston asked.

"Dr. Ralston, what fine coincidences this is meeting you," came the P'torra's voice.

The rear door from the room was securely locked and alarmed. If Ralston managed to batter it down, he'd alert everyone. Better to fight his way past the P'torra, if that proved necessary.

"Do not think so to do this unmentionable act," the P'torra cautioned. Ralston squarely faced the alien. Clutched in one of the well-fleshed, stubby-fingered hands the P'torra held a small box with two protruding wires.

"Not a lethal device, is it?" Ralston asked.

"I wish no harm to come to you, Doctor. Why for do you think so ill of me?"

Ralston tried to push past. He encountered blubbery P'torra flesh that didn't yield.

"I've got to get back to teach a class. Let me by."

"Your wondrous duties in teaching classrooms are suspended," answered the P'torra, unperturbed by Ralston's more aggressive attempts to push past and escape. "I mean you none harm."

"You manipulated the crowd well. I saw you with your impulse driver."

"I mean nothing against you personally," explained the P'torra. It smiled, revealing the twin rows of needle-sharp teeth. Without a decent nose, with the heavy folds of flesh on his face, the P'torra looked like something out of Ralston's worst nightmare.

Ralston tried to get past the P'torra again. The alien had wedged himself firmly into the narrow doorway, making escape almost impossible. Ralston stepped back and quickly sized up the alien. He had fought enough of them in the Nex-P'torra war to have an appreciation for how strong and hardy they were. Once, he had blasted off both legs of a P'torra field officer. That hadn't killed him. He had followed the officer for almost twenty kilometers; along the way the P'torra had killed four different varieties of creature with his bare hands. One of them, Ralston had heard, couldn't be killed with any armament short of a land-based energy cannon. When he'd finally found the P'torra officer, it took another five minutes of intense combat before the last whisper of life fled the fleshy alien body.

Ralston might respect them for their toughness, but he despised them for what they had done to the Nex—and what they continued to do on a half dozen other worlds.

"You think to slay me?" asked the P'torra.

"The thought never crossed my mind." Ralston knew how difficult such an act would be. He'd content himself with a disabling kick to the knees, a feint to one side and a quick escape in the opposite direction.

"I mean you none harm." The P'torra vented what Ralston knew to be laugh. He felt as if someone had scratched his soul with a diamond. "You are more much valuable to me as a symbol of the administration at Ilium University."

From outside the library, Ralston heard a student haranguing a crowd. He looked at the P'torra, who smiled even more wickedly.

"How did you know where to find me?" Ralston asked. Even as he asked, he knew. The answer burned brightly within him. He wanted verification, however.

"You are a popularly wanted professor, Dr. Ralston. All computer billings show their importance at some point in the University."

"You sidetracked the request at the comptroller's office," he said. This told Ralston more than he wanted to know. Not only did Salazar and the committee want to keep track of him, the University officials didn't care who was privy to that information. They wanted to write him off as quickly and quietly as possible. If the P'torra provided additional aid, so much the better.

"Such paranoia that is yours." The P'torra chuckled. "Many humans want to be sought out. Are you unlike them?"

Ralston kicked without any tensing of his muscles. The blow lacked real power but he'd aimed it accurately. He caught the P'torra on the side of his knee and brought the bulky alien

down. A second, harder kick disabled the P'torra. Ralston
lithely jumped over his victim and landed outside the hardcopy
room.

"Don't," Ralston said, such menace in his voice that the
P'torra stopped trying to reach out and grab his leg. Ralston
stepped away, out of any possible reach. "You say you don't
bear me any malice. It's not true for me. Remember that."

"There is no need for to remember such a memory, Dr.
Ralston," said the P'torra. "You will not long be at this University."

Ralston didn't want to blunder into the crowd gathering in
front of the library. He found a side exit, glanced around and
saw nothing but shadows and the insectlike winklights floating
along the paths and providing gentle illumination. Ralston
avoided the paths and kept to the darker areas. As he got to
the top of a small rise, he looked back down at the library
where the crowd gathered.

The words were lost in the distance, but not their intent.
The student leader on the steps made all the gestures appropriate
to a lynch mob. Ralston kept walking, wanting to find Druanna
Thorkkin and talk with her. But he knew that wasn't possible.
As much as he needed her, it wouldn't be fair for him to involve
her with the P'torra and his campaign of campus unrest. The
P'torra had made it quite clear that Ralston's every move was
being closely watched.

Ralston would have to do without a friend and consolation
this night. He spent many long hours studying the information
he had pulled from the University computer banks, integrating
this with what Westcott had told him.

After he had finished, Ralston needed a friend to confide
in even more. Never had he felt so alone.

"I've got to see Dr. Salazar right away. This is important,"
Ralston said, almost shouting. He'd gotten little sleep the night
before and his nerves were frayed from dodging the P'torra-
incited students around campus. He didn't want to deal with
underlings.

"I'm sure you think it is, Dr. Ralston," said Salazar's secretary, "but he is in conference."

Ralston chafed at the delay but saw no way to circumvent
the officious secretary. Few at the University had human sec-

retaries; most bureaucrats made do with automated systems. Salazar proved more status conscious, and flaunted his importance by hiring the man sitting and glaring at Ralston.

Ralston had to admit a human buffer proved more effective in most cases. Most people had been well enough trained to obey a mechanical command. Those few—like him—who hadn't, only a human barrier could stop.

After twenty minutes, three people left Salazar's office. Two of them Ralston recognized as Constance and Arturo de la Cruz. The third, a neatly dressed woman carrying a small legal case, had to be their attorney. The two de la Cruzes glared at Ralston but made no comment. The attorney didn't even notice him.

"You wanted something, Doctor?" called out Salazar.

"Something vital, Dr. Salazar."

"Very well," the man said tiredly. "But I can only give you a few minutes. This has been a busy day and it looks as if I'll be here until well past midnight. I'm to meet with University legal counsel at eleven hours."

Ralston glanced at the wall chronometer. That gave him less than ten minutes. He hurried into Salazar's office.

"What is it, Ralston? I've had about enough of you these past few days. I assume you recognized the brother and sister of the student you killed."

"I killed no one," Ralston said, hardly expecting more from Salazar. The man had already made up his mind on the matter. Ralston pushed aside such concerns for one he considered even greater. "Look at this."

Ralston dropped a block into Salazar's desk projector. Without asking permission, he turned it on. One wall filled with decorations faded away as the projection dominated.

"Westcott plotted this. A trajectory of some device past Alpha 3, past these other points—all novas. I believe that this device caused the decline of Alpha 3's civilization and was responsible for its eventual demise. And that it also caused these stars to go nova."

Ralston paused, then amended, "At least some of them might have gone nova. I haven't had time to check on the possibility that some are naturally occurring. This one—the one in orange—seems to be of a type to naturally evolve into a nova." He pointed out Chen's 1054 "guest star." "The others might have been triggered."

"What is all this rubbish?" demanded Salazar. "Are you totally insane?"

"Consider this, Dr. Salazar. An object passes by a solar system. Somehow it causes instabilities to occur, in societies, in the stellar processes, in individuals."

"You're trying to tell me this imagined device of yours is responsible for de la Cruz's death?"

"I don't know," Ralston said honestly, "but it's possible that, by entering one of the dioramas depicting the final days of Alpha 3, he absorbed part of the madness that destroyed their culture."

"Absurd."

"I thought so, too, but this all fits together."

"What produced this alleged device?"

"Maybe not *what* but *who*. It might be a messenger from some other race trying to contact intelligences. Back in pre-space days, Earth sent out satellites with messages."

"Preposterous. Both that and your theory."

"This might not be a friendly warning. It might be a weapon. Or it might be a naturally occurring field somehow orbiting through the plane of the galaxy. I don't know what it is or its possible origin, but its results are obvious."

"Not to me."

"Here," Ralston said, moving to a new projection. "Something Westcott said to me sent me off on a search of University records. Three centuries ago on Earth mathematicians formulated what they called the equations of chaos." Ralston cut off Salazar's angry response. "These equations were supposed to predict what appears to be random behavior. The formation of weather patterns, radioactive decay, electronic component failure."

"And?" Salazar said sarcastically. "What else?"

"They also worked to predict the course of epilepsy in humans. That and computer component failure have much in common."

Salazar rocked back in his chair and stared at Ralston for a few seconds, then said, "You want me to believe this mythical device, artificial or naturally occurring, went speeding by Alpha 3 more than ten thousand years ago and left as its legacy seizures of the sort that claimed Citizen de la Cruz?"

"It's possible."

"It's ridiculous."

"There might be another problem, Dr. Salazar. The legacy, as you called it, might not be limited to humans. I strongly believe that it has caused the Alpha primary to become prenova."

"People go crazy, stars blow up, is there anything else this mythical machine of yours does?"

"What other natural processes might be destabilized?" asked Ralston. "Can it cause war? Devastating weather patterns?" He spoke off the top of his head. Even as he mentioned the weather patterns, he remembered the diorama pictures of Alpha 3 and the current mudball. This change, too, might have been caused by the device's passing.

"This leap of faith on your part is incredible, Ralston. You have not one shred of evidence for your wild claims, and I don't believe them for an instant. I must assume that you seek a scapegoat for your own negligence. Why de la Cruz died, I can't say. But I can and do say that you are responsible."

"What if I'm right? This device is still roving through the galaxy. We have no way of determining which direction along the trajectory Westcott plotted it might be traveling."

"Correlate with time of occurrence," snapped Salazar.

"We are talking about *random* events. This thing might interfere with what we think of as random, spontaneous events. Think of the power, Dr. Salazar! To be able to control radioactive decay—or to predict it. To predict weather exactly."

Salazar stared out his window. An unexpected rain shower dampened the campus. Even with extensive weather satellite forecasts, mistakes were made, usually on a daily basis.

Ralston saw how the man weakened at the notion of something financially beneficial for the University of Ilium.

"If nothing else, if I can't unlock the secret, there is always the thought projector inside the dioramas. The later ones might be tainted with this uncertainty, this randomness or forced order—call it what you will—but the earlier ones aren't."

"The University could certainly use an influx of fresh funds," mused Salazar.

"I need permission to return to Alpha 3 immediately."

"Out of the question. There are preliminary hearings in the de la Cruz matter. And we cannot afford funding for such a venture on your part."

"We dare not wait. The Alpha primary might go nova at any instant. Seconds might be vital."

"No," Salazar said firmly. "I will present your request to the full committee, but under no circumstance could we authorize your return until after the de la Cruz situation is satisfactorily resolved."

"Time is running out," said Ralston. He pulled the block from the projector and slid it across Salazar's desk. "Study this more carefully. And think what might happen if we don't find out what caused an entire civilization to self-destruct." Ralston paused, then said, "Can you imagine not learning what controls such chaos, what gives it order and uses it for destructive purposes?" He glanced dramatically out the window. Warm, syrupy sunlight broke through the cloud cover.

"Can you imagine *our* sun exploding?"

Ralston turned and left Salazar's office. He didn't know if the administrator had been convinced of the seriousness of the problem, but Ralston knew one thing: He had certainly convinced himself.

THIRTEEN

"I'M BEING FOLLOWED," the seedy man said, nervously looking around for pursuers.

"Don't worry," Michael Ralston assured the man. "You're safe. It's me they want."

"The P'torra?"

Ralston nodded. He hadn't had an instant's rest since the abortive riot in front of the office building. Students came to the University of Ilium for many reasons. Some fled here to be away from their family for the first time in their lives. Others genuinely sought education. A few wanted something to do and had nothing better to occupy their time. And then Ralston considered the P'torra in this quagmire of half-realized dreams and frustrations. The alien seemed interested in learning—but what he studied!

Everywhere Ralston turned, the P'torra stood with his impulse driver in hand, tallying up human responses, suggesting alternatives to his pawns, finding new tactics to drive the crowd to a frenzy. By the time the alien left Novo Terra and returned to his home world, he would be expert in psychological techniques.

That he might be one of the select few who had learned what he'd come to the University of Ilium to learn didn't keep Ralston from cursing him.

"He finds me convenient because of my beliefs," Ralston said. "I need to know your progress." The sudden shift in topic took the nervous man by surprise.

"What? Oh, the starship. It's ready. In orbit. But it'll cost you dearly. Pilot's got expenses. Have to avoid the authorized traffic. A lot is going into orbit now. Manufacturing season for the orbiting factories. And the patrols might think you're smuggling something, too. Dangerous."

Ralston had withdrawn his life savings. It barely covered this man's finder's fee for the starship. But Ralston wasn't above using his University account to the maximum. He hadn't been shut off completely—apparently Salazar hadn't considered Ralston's drawing on funds a possibility. Even with this and Druanna's loan, Ralston found himself short.

Leonore Disa covered that and furnished the master supervisor he so desperately needed on Muckup.

It paid to have rich, committed graduate students willing to take risks. Ralston smiled. It didn't hurt to have the hottest discovery of all time, either—and Leonore Disa separated from her lover on that planet.

"Take the shuttle pod up at half past midnight. You'll star out an hour later. If you don't show, everything's off. No second chances, no refunds."

"I understand," Ralston said. "Is everything on board now?"

A quick nod was the only answer.

"And Leonore? Is she already aboard?" Ralston still had reservations about allowing her to accompany him, but the need for skilled hands at the machinery outweighed the danger. He was gambling everything. Leonore Disa might die, but if she did, Ralston wouldn't be in any worse trouble than he was now—he'd be dead alongside her.

Ralston snorted. He doubted that was the proper way of looking at their situation. Their atoms would be intermixed with the superheated gases of the outer edge of an expanding nova. No bodies, no remains, no trace except for a few energetic protons, neutrons and electrons. All his worries would be over in a flash.

But that wouldn't happen. A better conclusion to this reck-lessness would be proof of his theories concerning Alpha 3.

Again came the quick jerking movement of the head Ralston interpreted to mean the man assented. Leonore and the equipment spun in orbit above Novo Terra. He had to join them by half past midnight or the entire mad venture came to an end.

Ralston said nothing to the man as he turned and walked off. To have spoken even a simple good-bye would have triggered paranoias best left untouched. The friendly environment of the University campus spread around Ralston like a green ocean wave, interrupted here and there by buildings. But whatever serenity he'd felt here before had evaporated. He walked quickly toward the administration building. With luck he could catch Salazar and the committee before they got down to serious discussion of how best to remove him from their school.

"Dr. Ralston, wait!" cried the secretary as he hurried past. Ralston didn't slow down. He got through the door and had it closed before the secretary could stop him. Inside the room, a half dozen heads swiveled to see who intruded on their deliberations.

"Dr. Ralston, this is a closed meeting," said Salazar in an icy tone that meant they'd been discussing the termination of a professor: Dr. Michael Lewis Ralston.

Ralston held on to the door handle and prevented the secretary from entering. Muscles stood out in thick cords on his arms as he applied more and more pressure to keep the door shut.

"I only need a few minutes of your time, Doctor."

"Very well." Though Salazar seemed resigned to such intrusions, he didn't appear to be receptive to anything Ralston might say.

Ralston released the door handle and abruptly stepped to one side. The secretary slammed through the suddenly unresisting door and fell facedown on the floor. The sheepish expression and mumbled apology covered Ralston's move across the room to seat himself before the committee that would decide his fate. Salazar waved the secretary back to his post outside.

"I'm not here to plead my case," said Ralston. "Rather, I'd like a firm commitment from you to exploit the valuable technology we found on Alpha 3."

"What?" Salazar frowned.

"After the de la Cruz matter is settled, and I am certain it will be terminated in my favor, I'd like permission to return to Alpha 3 to expedite removal of the technology."

"This is premature, Ralston."

"Not really, Dr. Salazar. It takes time to get even a skeleton expedition put together." One of the committee snickered at the small joke. Ralston gratefully acknowledged and rushed on. "It'll have to be done quickly, in and out before the nova."

"I appreciate your eagerness, Doctor, but . . ."

"All I'm asking is for the committee to give a tentative agreement that, should I be cleared of all charges in the de la Cruz unpleasantness, that I be allowed to return to Alpha 3."

"The telepathic projection device might prove a boon," murmured one of the committee members Ralston didn't recognize. "A financial banquet from which the University might feed for many years."

"Remember the Vegan spider steel," another said. "We missed out on that entirely. We dare not permit another financial opportunity to pass us by."

"Exactly," Ralston gushed. "We owe it to the University to exploit this discovery to the fullest." He had their attention, and he knew what Salazar would say next. Ralston almost laughed when it came.

"Dr. Ralston, I'm sure you'll agree that this discovery is too, uh, significant to be bypassed, should you become mired down in litigation over Citizen de la Cruz's demise."

Ralston surprised Salazar by volunteering what the man hinted at. "If such occurs, I'd be willing to allow others to exploit my find. For the good of the University, of course."

Salazar sat speechless, taken back. Archaeologists, like all researchers, had insufferable egos when it came to protecting their discoveries. Ralston casually passed it over to another simply because he discounted any possible involvement in Yago de la Cruz's death. The wicked smile of triumph crossing Salazar's face couldn't be stopped.

Ralston didn't mind. He needed this agreement, no matter the price in emotional terms.

"Let it be so recorded," said Salazar. He punched a button hidden on the desktop. "There. If there's nothing else, Ralston, please excuse us. We have considerable business to attend to before the public hearing tomorrow." Salazar glanced at a screen out of Ralston's line of sight. "Be here for the opening recitation of preliminary statements at eight hours, sharp."

"Yes, sir." Ralston stood. "Thank you for your confidence. I'm sure we'll be free of this quickly."

He left, not caring that Salazar smirked and that the secretary shot daggers at him with his eyes. Ralston didn't slow until he came to a computer console down the hall in the administration building. While this sort of larceny required quiet for total concentration, Ralston knew he didn't have much time. And to return to his office and the console there might take too long.

One of his students had long ago showed him how minutes from all administration meetings were filed in the University data banks. Every five minutes the voice record dumped into memory. In this way, not more than that five minutes could be lost, should an equipment malfunction occur, yet unwanted or unacceptable testimony could be deleted before permanent entry.

Ralston intercepted the agreement as it went into a buffer. He worked quickly, perhaps too quickly. Sweat beaded his forehead. He might miss editing something significant, but he didn't have the benefit of infinite time to work.

Ralston leaned back and let out a pent-up breath. The effort looked crude to his eye, but then he had been present in the room and knew what really had been said. A deletion here, a changed word there and the computer record now authorized Ralston to leave for Alpha 3, with no mention made of the de la Cruz hearing or sending someone in his stead to the find. Ralston pushed the transmit key and the screen blinked clear, the altered record now a permanent part of University records.

Ralston tried to remember all his student had said about access to other files. He hadn't paid that much attention to what he had considered little more than a prank. Now he struggled to call up the University vidnews account and leave a message. Ralston failed, but he did find a way to send a memo to the reporter who had tried to interview him. He struggled to remember her name. He finally addressed it simply to Citizen Tranton, unable to call back her first name.

"Dr. Ralston," came the voice that dug into his consciousness like a nail pounded into wood.

"What do you want?" he asked harshly. The P'torra moved around to a point where he might view the screen. Ralston hastily punched the transmit button again; the text of the falsified interview now went into the reporter's file. The University vidnews would pick up the story since anything dealing with Ralston constituted front-page news. And Ralston believed that it would be a banner headline because he had emphasized the financial returns possible to the University from the telepathic projector he'd supposedly promised to bring back.

Fail and he might be the butt of jokes. Ralston vowed that wouldn't happen, either—he wouldn't go up in a puff of plasma nor would he let one tidbit of knowledge slip through his fingers.

"You call up to the others of your department of archaeology?" the P'torra asked.

"I've been leaving dirty notes for all the female students." Ralston swung away from the computer console and tried to get past the P'torra. The alien blocked him.

"This I do not understand. How can computer memos be soiled?"

Ralston glanced past the P'torra, expecting to see another mob forming. Wherever the alien went, trouble followed. But not this time. If anything, this worried Ralston even more.

"Excuse me. I've got business elsewhere." When the alien didn't move, Ralston took a half step back. Seeing that the professor might unleash another attack, the P'torra moved. Ralston thought he noticed a slight jerkiness to the movement in the alien's knee. He hoped so. But they were tough. It'd take more than a swift kick to a joint to disable the P'torra.

"Dr. Ralston, we should gather for food-eating and speak to each other."

Ralston almost vomited. The idea of eating with a P'torra nauseated him. He walked out the side door of the administration building, then wandered aimlessly through the campus, no destination in mind. All he wanted to do was walk off the nervousness that had accumulated while he altered the computer files.

The soft green of the grass, the blue skies, and caressing breezes took the edge off his tension, but Ralston knew that he couldn't linger to savor them. If Salazar called back the minutes of the meeting, he'd notice immediately how they had been falsified. Since the only one with a motive for such a crime was Ralston, it wouldn't be hard finding the guilty party.

Ralston couldn't miss the late-night deadline for starring back to Alpha 3. He looked up into the morning sky and saw nothing, but somewhere in a low parking orbit spun the starship that meant his future.

He turned and retraced his steps, then made a sudden right angle turn. Shielded by a row of shrubs Ralston waited. The P'torra came waddling along, head swiveling back and forth on the thick neck as he vainly sought his quarry. Ralston had no idea what the alien wanted, but it wasn't likely to be beneficial.

He considered removing the alien permanently, then immediately discarded the notion. Killing the P'torra might be gratifying, but it only raised the ugly specter of police intervention. They might close down all his possible escape routes, especially if the University vidnews released the story on how Salazar authorized Ralston to return to Alpha 3 immediately.

While he couldn't read it at this distance, he stared across the Quad at one of the vidnews kiosks. All he saw was the slow march of lines up and off the screen top; the words weren't distinct. Ralston hurried on until he topped a rise and looked down at the gymnasium. He hated to involve Druanna Thorkkin but had no other choice now.

Trying not to appear as if he thought everyone on Novo Terra chased him, Ralston went down the hill toward the large building.

"I suppose that will have to keep me happy until you get back," Druanna Thorkkin said. She rolled over in bed and stared at Ralston. He paced to and fro, then stopped and smiled at her. Ralston bent over and lightly kissed her.

"I don't know what I'd do without you, Dru," he said. "You and your optimism."

"What optimism?" she said, sitting up. "I'm a realist. I look at you and what do I see? Someone whose drive won't let him stop until he wins. It comes out when you fence. You're relentless."

"Is that another way of telling me I'm a better fencer than you are?"

"It's *why* you are. I'm quicker, but it doesn't matter. You don't give in. Besides, you owe me money."

Ralston peered out the window of Druanna's small, quaintly

furnished home and saw the sun setting. Less than four hours until the deadline for reaching the starship. By early morning, Novo Terra reckoning, he'd be returning to Alpha 3.

"You set goals well and you've got the tenacity to carry through. This isn't ego-building on my part. It's just the way you are. Don't get me wrong. I like it."

"You don't think Alpha Prime will go nova and turn me into a cinder?" Ralston only half joked.

"It wouldn't dare. Not until you've stripped everything you want from that muddy planet." Druanna rose and began rummaging through her closet. "Can't find a thing. Maybe I ought to get that robot valet I saw advertised on the vid."

"You'd hate it. I tried one and it organized me out of my home. Everything was in its place. Awful," said Ralston.

"For you, that must be purest hell. Your place always looks as if you intend for it to be the primary dig site for archaeologists a thousand years from now. You people do revel in debris, don't you?" She selected and quickly dressed. Ralston watched with appreciation and a little sadness.

Accepting. That summed up Druanna Thorkkin's attitude well. She made no demands, yet she gave willingly. And in that giving lay the true strength of their relationship. Ralston never—quite—dared deny her anything. It wasn't—quite—freely given on his part, but he owed it to her. That always struck him as unfair. Dru deserved more from him. But it wasn't in him to give it.

She accepted that, too.

"You still have that night class?" he asked.

"The medieval lit course? Hardly. Registration for it has been falling off drastically. Who wants to read Hawthorne and Tolstoy and Unamuno when they can read the moderns?"

"You do."

"I'm weird. Just like you. We're of a kind, Michael. Both of us are mired in the past. Your past just happens to be further in the past than mine."

"If you don't have the class, mind taking me for a ride?"

"I'll take you for a ride anytime, bucko," she said.

"Might get nasty."

"I can handle it." From her joking response Ralston knew she didn't believe him. He had never been more serious, however. A hundred things might have betrayed him—a thousand.

He had no idea what sources of information the P'torra had. He didn't even know the alien's motives in making him the scapegoat for the campus unrest. It might go much deeper than trying to eliminate P'torra opposition.

Salazar might have discovered the tampering with the committee minutes. The University vidnews might have already run the story. If Salazar saw that, he'd definitely have the campus security force looking for Ralston.

"You did something pretty outrageous today, didn't you?" asked Druanna.

"You call what we did outrageous? Why, I've heard that on Elysium 2, they . . ."

"You know what I mean, Michael."

He told her how he'd tampered with the records. Druanna smiled broadly and asked, "How did you do it, now? I want to know. This can come in handy."

"I've put Salazar in a bad spot," he said. "It'll look as if he authorized my departure *before* the de la Cruz hearing. If I come back with the telepathy gadget, I'm a hero and they have to give me medals."

"And if you don't, your ass is grass, anyway. Nice move. You could have taught the ancient generals a thing or two, Michael."

"I've studied more than how to rob graves. *Vom Kriege* is one of my favorite books. Can we get going?" He glanced out the window again. Dusk had hardened into night. In the sky he saw a half-dozen slowly moving points. Some were information satellites, others starships in orbit waiting for cargos or passengers. He had no idea which was going to be his ticket back to Muckup.

A pounding on the door startled him.

"No, Michael, not that way," Druanna said when he tried to force open the window. "It's permanently sealed. This way."

"We're not going to be able to hide," he said. "They'll scan the place with IR sensors. Even a single wall between us won't . . ." His voice trailed off when he saw a staircase hidden in one closet and going below ground level. The woman impatiently gestured for him to be quiet. He hurried down the spiraling stairs. Druanna closed the closet door and rushed after him.

"That way. A tunnel out to my flyer."

"How'd you ever come to have this built?" he asked.

"I dug it myself. Pretty good work, eh? See the supports?"

"But why?"

"You pace. I need to be doing something more substantial and more private. So I dig. Got fed up with a garden that kept dying and thought this'd be a positively medieval touch for the house. Keeps me out of the rain, too."

Ralston quickly ascended another spiral staircase and came out in a small shed not five meters from Druanna's flyer. A man stood guard beside it.

"Now what?" she whispered.

Ralston never hesitated. All the combat training given him by the Nex rushed back. He strode out, planted his feet, and drove his fist only a few centimeters—into the man's left kidney. The guard gasped and fell face-forward onto the ground, unconscious before he hit.

"Who does he belong to?" asked Druanna. Ralston jerked her into the flyer. He didn't care. He had to reach the launch site or be left behind.

He seated himself at the controls, warmed up the engine, and complimented Druanna on how well she maintained the machine. He swung the flyer around and sent it quietly following the buried induction cable to the main road. He glanced behind and saw a half-dozen figures rushing from Druanna's home.

He turned the controls to max. The acceleration flattened them in their seats.

"You always were a dangerous one," she said.

"And this is getting too dangerous for you," he said. "Take the controls. Keep it at full speed. You know the Estrellita Launch Bay?"

"The tiny field outside the main port? I think so."

"I have a shuttle pod waiting for me there. When we get near it, I want you to slow down, I'll jump out, then you speed up and just drive around."

"You think they're following us?" She made a motion with her head indicating those who'd been in her home.

"Not a bad working hypothesis," he said. "You decoy them. I'll be off for Alpha 3."

"Some people have all the fun."

"I'll bring back lots of photos."

"How I spent my summer vacation," Druanna said sarcastically. "You never take me anywhere."

"You wouldn't like it on Muckup. Too wet." He leaned over and kissed her. Before she could say another word, he pointed. "There's the turn where I want off."

"This slow enough?"

"Have to do. See you in a few months." With that Ralston threw open the door and heaved himself out. He hit, rolled, and smashed hard against a tree. For several seconds all he heard was the ringing in his ears. He shook himself and got painfully to his feet.

Druanna's flyer had already vanished down the road. At top speed she might already be three or four kilometers distant. He oriented himself and started walking.

Before he'd gone two hundred meters he broke into a run. The resonant hum of at least two flyers broke the stillness of the night. If they had figured out what he was up to, they'd know he was headed for the shuttle launch site. He couldn't risk their continuing on after Druanna's flyer. He ran even faster when he saw the launch lights ahead.

Gasping for breath, Ralston leaned heavily against a shed. Through the pounding of his pulse in his head he heard the magnetic hum of flyers. They hadn't been decoyed away. That was all right with Ralston; that meant Druanna had gotten away cleanly.

Some wind regained, Ralston sprinted hard for the stubby cargo ship sitting in the middle of the launch apron. The gigantic laser beneath it hissed with escaping coolant gases and crackled with the ultrahigh voltages.

"Get it ready for launch," he shouted as he ran. Ralston took a second to look over his shoulder. The first flyer grounded and three men clambered out.

"What's going on?" asked the field tech. "Look, if you're running from the police, forget this launch. I'm not getting paid enough to get myself rehabbed."

"They're not police," gasped Ralston. "University prank. They're supposed to kidnap me as part of an initiation. I'm their archaeology professor."

"Yeah, he'd mentioned you were one of those." The man frowned as he worked through the possibilities. "Then we'll call the police. They shouldn't do that to you. Not unless you want to play along."

"Launch the damned thing!"

"All right, all right. We'll show them. You're going to be in orbit before they know what's happening."

A loud klaxon signaled all off the field. Ralston dived through the door and flopped onto an acceleration couch. The pilot silently waited in the cockpit for takeoff, oblivious to all that went on below.

Ralston screwed his eyes tightly shut, even though it was impossible for him to see the launcher light. The sudden takeoff crushed the air from his still straining lungs. The laser repeatedly fired, hammering against the ceramic refractory base of the shuttle pod. The only sounds Ralston heard were the rush of air past the hull, the pilot's monotone recitation of launch data, and the pounding of his own heart.

When the shuttle's guidance rockets cut in, Ralston knew he'd escaped. Novo Terra would be left behind and Alpha 3's secrets would be unlocked. He tried to relax but found himself too keyed up.

Alpha 3's secrets would be his!

FOURTEEN

"THIS ISN'T WHAT I thought he'd arrange," said Michael Ralston after he had boarded the starship. This vessel was easily twice the size of the one he had starred on previously to Alpha 3.

"A few additional arrangements were made," Leonore Disa told him, smiling. "I thought you might appreciate this more than the garbage can your mysterious friend had arranged."

"He's no friend," Ralston said. "But I paid him good money. You didn't spook him, did you? He's paranoid about anything out of the ordinary happening during a deal."

"Then he'll approve of the change in plans." Leonore gestured that Ralston was to follow her. They went to a lounge area—a lounge!—and peered up at a small vidscreen showing the cockpit where the pilot toiled in preflight checks.

"This isn't possible," Ralston said. "He couldn't have gotten a ship this large." Suspiciously, Ralston asked the woman, "Your father furnished it, didn't he? Does he know?"

"Daddy doesn't know any more than I told him. Which isn't

149

much. Relax, Michael. This is all legal, unlike that other starship." She pointed to an inset in the screen. A small cargo ship showed in it, hardly more than a dot, even with the electronic magnification.

Before Ralston could say anything, the pilot's voice came over a speaker. "Flight Control's just canceled the cargo ship's launch request. What do you think's on that monstrosity? Some members of that religious cult who go around blowing up churches?"

"That doesn't matter," Leonore said into a small microphone. "What's *not* on it matters more. Hurry with the shift."

"Even if FC tells us to wait?" The pilot's voice quivered with excitement.

"It might be best if you experienced some difficulty hearing such orders," Leonore said, skirting a direct answer. The pilot's face almost glowed at the intrigue and challenge.

"We'll be on Alpha 3 in three weeks," he promised. Ralston watched in fascination as the pilot's hands glided over the controls. A gentle nudge told of acceleration pulling them to a higher orbit.

"This is an Interstellar Computronics ship?" Ralston asked Leonore. "And your father doesn't know what his daughter's doing?"

"Something like that. Don't worry so. You're sounding as if it's not important to get back to Alpha 3."

"Three weeks?"

"This ship is faster than most. Daddy always wanted me to use my own initiative. What'll he do to me, anyway? Spank me? I own fifteen percent of IC, and he knows I'd give him a hard time at the next stockholders' meeting. So relax, Michael. It's all right."

Ralston didn't have it in his heart to complain. The less time in transit, the more time he could spend gathering information on Muckup. That muddy ball spinning through space had such a short lifetime now. He wanted to be its biographer, to find every secret of its people, to know it all!

If some small deceptions had to be made along the way, so be it. Hadn't he already altered University records, released a vidnews story to the effect that Salazar had authorized this return? What was it to him if Leonore lied her way into a faster, more luxurious starship than he could possibly afford through connections who survived at the very fringes of Novo Terran law?

"They've definitely impounded the cargo ship," the pilot said over the speaker. "Something about contraband? Maybe so, yeah, verd, definitely. This is hot. Prepare for preshift maneuvers. Starting sequencing . . . now!"

The ship had attained an orbit at six planetary diameters. Rockets cut in and slammed Ralston back onto his couch. The ship headed into emptiness where the pilot had marked an imaginary takeoff spot. Once there, they would star for Alpha 3.

"How long?" he asked Leonore.

"The pilot's the best. We'll shift within a few hours."

"Good," said Ralston, settling down, knowing this would be the last weight he'd feel for close to a month. But the trip would be a busy one this time. No work on an archaeology textbook that'd never see publication. He had equipment to prepare. And he and Leonore had to work out a schedule to maximize what they could accomplish.

Time pressed in on him. But Ralston smiled. He felt more alive than he had since finding the dioramas. The committee meetings were behind him, confronting de la Cruz's death something to be postponed, all that he hated most either deferred or finished. Everything that lay ahead was what he loved most: discovery.

"Can't he hurry?" Ralston asked. He floated through the lounge area, trailing equipment like a mechanical hydra. He needed several more weeks to finish programming the master supervisor, but he found himself even more anxious to land on Alpha 3's muddy surface.

"He came in on target," Leonore said. She seemed to be able to read the pilot's instruments. Ralston wondered if she might not be a starship pilot herself, but he didn't ask. Too many other things to know, too much else to do.

"Two days?" he pressed.

"I'm certain."

"Citizen Disa," came the pilot's voice. Throughout the three-week trip, the pilot had remained in his quarters. Only twice had Ralston seen him drifting through the ship—he counted these as the peculiar moments. Pilots tended to be clannish and reclusive, never dealing directly with their passengers. Even on the longest trips, those lasting several months, pilots segregated themselves from their passengers.

"Yes?"

"Got a Dr. Bernssen on the com. You want to talk to him?"

"Yes!" Ralston both heard the delighted excitement in Leonore's voice and saw the reaction. Her cheeks flushed and her space-induced paleness vanished.

"What are you doing back here?" came Nels Bernssen's querulous voice. "We're in the middle of a heavy-particle solar storm alert. Might come at any time."

Ralston saw the pilot stiffen at the warning and reach over to tap a detector. The dull amber glow on the instrument's face indicated only moderate danger, he guessed.

"We'll land within a day," Leonore said. "Aren't you glad that I'm back, Nels?"

"No! It's getting dangerous. Radiation levels are up. Solar instability is increasing again. There might be only days left."

Ralston cursed under his breath.

"You're not leaving, are you?"

"Not for a while. But it can't be much longer. Weeks, maybe, days are more likely. You were safe. Why'd you come back?"

"We have work to do, too," she said primly. Ralston saw how irritated Leonore was at the lack of warm reception on Bernssen's part.

"Let me," Ralston said, reaching to the microphone. "Dr. Bernssen, we can't let the discovery go up in a flash of nova, but we're not suicidal, either. If you can give me a guarantee that the star will explode before we can unload and work a few more days, we'll turn around and go back to Novo Terra."

"Do it," said Bernssen.

"You can guarantee we'll never get even a few days' further exploration done?"

"Hell, I can't *guarantee* that, but the star's going to blow soon. Why the hell else do you think *I'm* here?"

"Please let us know when you're preparing to leave. We'll depart then, too."

"Leonore's going to be in danger," Bernssen protested.

"So are you, Nels. Your work's important. Mine is, too!" the woman said angrily.

Bernssen mumbled something that got lost in the heavy solar storm—induced static. "Land, then," he said. "I've got to tell Dr. Rasmussen about it, though."

"Please do," said Ralston. "We'll want to keep in close communication." Ralston relinquished the microphone and kicked away a few feet.

The lowered air pressure robbed him of the words Leonore spoke, but he saw her lips moving. He read, "I love you, Nels." She then tossed the microphone away and went back to work on one of their ultrasonic cleaning heads, as if nothing had happened.

But Ralston saw that the glow in her cheeks remained.

"You're out of your chinging minds," complained Nels Bernssen. The burly solar physicist heaved one of the bulky instrument-laden crates aside where a small robot worked to pull off the sides and ready the equipment inside.

"Thanks for helping us, Nels. I appreciate it." Leonore stood on tiptoe and lightly kissed him on the cheek.

"You're going to get yourselves killed, and all for what? A few lousy pictures that wouldn't be of interest to anybody at the University, even in a tridee play."

"This isn't fiction. It's an entire culture. We can't let it be destroyed."

"It's all going up, no matter what we do."

"It's important," insisted Leonore, pausing to wipe sweat from her eyes. "Just as your work's important."

Ralston knew that line of logic would fail. To Bernssen, nothing could be as important. Ralston had to smile to himself. Each researcher thought their particular line of inquiry was the most vital. Ego entered into it, but often that fed genius and produced breakthroughs. Intuition as much as logic produced the important discoveries. He had been lucky with this one. Luck. Intuition. Logic. All elements of good research. And maybe the most important part, the researcher's absolute conviction in the project.

Ralston looked up at the sky. Through the fluffy clouds forming up for the afternoon's rainstorm, he saw shimmering veils that floated and vanished, darted about and formed thicker blankets in what ought to be clear sky.

"So you noticed it, eh?" asked Bernssen.

"What is it?"

"You've never seen an aurora?"

"In the middle of the day?"

"That," said Bernssen grimly, "is what worries all of us. The electrical activity in the atmosphere is growing more and more intense each day. At night, the sky's lit up like a neon sign. Pretty, when you can see it through the clouds."

"Did Dr. Rasmussen get the block I sent over this morning after we landed?"

Bernssen nodded. "The pilot delivered it. What's in it?"

"An explanation for all this, I think," Ralston said.

Bernssen didn't reply. He would hardly believe an archaeologist held such knowledge.

"It's all chaotic behavior," Ralston went on. "Induced, I think, by something that passed by Alpha 3 over ten thousand years ago. The weather's different now, the native populace died out, their sun's exploding."

Bernssen looked on all this as another proof that Ralston had become quite insane.

"Stay out of the direct sunlight, if you can," Bernssen advised. "The proton storms that hit now and again get through even the atmosphere and give quite a jolt. We'll give you warning on those so you can get underground. Justine thinks the atmosphere will boil off before too much longer."

"All the more reason to get to work," Ralston said. He stared at the master controller. The complex device could drive a thousand different machines. They had only a few dozen. He flipped the switch. Grinding noises from outside the plastic shelter told of the automated collector equipment beginning operation. Ralston glanced outside and saw the automated probes vanishing through the copper door.

But for all the spectroscopic analyses, for all the photos and probings, the real work lay with him and Leonore. The dioramas "spoke" only to the human mind.

Ralston waited for Leonore to bid her farewells to Bernssen in private before he went outside to join her. Bernssen's land crawler vanished behind a brown cloud of mud and spray and soon passed beyond limits of hearing.

Leonore sighed. "He's really upset with me for coming back. Nels said that the weather patterns are totally unpredictable now. No matter how much their meteorologist studies the satellite photos, he can't guess what'll happen for longer than a few hours."

"Chaos is accelerating," Ralston mused. "It's almost as if it were a virus that's finally spread throughout the body, destroying all systems."

"Or an echo that's finally returned," she said. "As much as your theory bothers me, it seems to fit what we know of Alpha 3. Their decline came too fast."

"The epilepsy epidemic is a strong argument that I'm right. Such an affliction couldn't have been caused by an ordinary disease and gone undetected. The evidence points to the natives as being fairly advanced in medicine."

"It's almost as if it were a capricious act of God," Leonore said. "He reached out His finger and touched the world, and its people died. And then its biome died. And then the sun."

"I think I interested Westcott enough in the problem to give it a few minutes' thought. He'll be trying to track the path of whatever it is that passed by. A device, I'm calling it. I refuse to believe such a chaotic field might exist naturally."

"Do you think it was a weapon that got away from the natives?"

"I think it's much older. The dioramas we've examined show them to be at peace for some time. I think the device came through on a more cosmic journey. I hope Westcott can pinpoint where it might have started—and where it went."

"Went?" Leonore's question hung in the air.

"I don't think it stayed here. It went on. Somewhere."

Leonore looked up into the overcast sky and shuddered. Lightning bolts of unimaginable proportions leaped from cloud to cloud and the first hints of rain began, virgas trailing down from the sky and drawing lacy fingers across the muddy terrain. She squinted at the sudden flashes, then turned to the supervisor and made a few minor adjustments.

"Static electricity's a problem," she said, not wanting to confront the idea of chaos forcing itself on any world she knew. "But we can compensate. Got it grounded pretty well."

Ralston nodded. They had set the data collection equipment in motion. Now they—he—had to do the rest. Ralston silently gestured for Leonore to pick up her camera and join him underground.

He'd have to selectively pick which dioramas to enter and

which to avoid. After all, Ralston wanted as much information as possible—and without ending up like the natives. Or Yago de la Cruz.

"The weather's driving me wild," Leonore Disa said. "How do you stand it?"

"I don't try," Ralston said. "I ignore it. He weaved from lack of sleep and from entering and experiencing twelve of the dioramas in the past planetary day. For a little over seventeen hours he had been swept back in time to an alien world, a world filled with birdlike natives and strange rituals and thought patterns—and he had *lived* their lives and learned the lessons they taught to their young. Ralston wobbled a bit, then sank down. One of the supervisor's data probes beeped. He moved out of its way. It hummed in contentment and entered the diorama he had just vacated.

"It's not getting any of the impressions I did, is it?" he asked. Ralston closed his eyes and wished for a month's sleep. But too much remained to be done. The threat of the nova hung over him like a sharp sword on a weakening thread.

Leonore didn't have to check the supervisor block circuits to know the answer. She shook her head.

Ralston looked along the corridor. Hundreds more of the dioramas remained. He increasingly felt the pressures of time. Justine Rasmussen had called twice to check on them, to urge them to leave. Nels Bernssen had called three more times. Ralston appreciated their solicitude but hated the interruptions.

The last call, however, had worn at him the most. Dr. Rasmussen claimed that the weather patterns had turned completely chaotic. Some sections between the solar physics site and the underground museum had been flooded to the point that travel might be impossible, even with the crawlers.

"There's so many to go," Leonore said, almost wistfully. "Can we make any progress at all?"

"You're still worried about lingering effects, aren't you?" he asked. Ralston thought his graduate assistant had summed it up well when she said that echoes of the cause had finally returned and were now being heard. Echoes of chaos, he mused. The primary cause of such disorder had passed ten thousand years ago, killing Alpha 3's populace, but the final result only now became apparent.

Ralston reached out and a static charge leaped from his finger to one of the IR probes. The robot flinched, as if it were human. He knew the master supervisor corrected current levels internally in the probe to keep the data uncompromised.

"I think that the natives carried the seeds of destruction within them. Whatever caused the epilepsy in de la Cruz must have been present in their population, also. Their telepathic projector transmitted it—can still transmit it."

"Pick the wrong scene to examine and you'll end up like de la Cruz. Not a cheerful notion," said Leonore.

"Any luck on removing the scenes and maintaining the projection?" The primary task, as he saw it, was not to personally examine as many of the dioramas as he could but to find a method of removing them intact and keeping them workable. The IC starship in orbit around Muckup had ample cargo space for dozens of the dioramas.

"Some," said Leonore. "The supervisor is still analyzing the strengths of various EM fields. Unusual intensity readings point to a possible mechanism being in the walls and in the figures themselves. We . . ."

The beeping of the com unit interrupted her. Almost angrily, Ralston grabbed it and snapped, "What is it?"

"Michael?" came Justine Rasmussen's voice. The interference caused by the lightning, the intense aurora, and the solar radiation bathing their com satellite made her sound weak, vulnerable. Ralston softened somewhat. The fatigue wore on him as much as his frustration at not making more progress.

"Yes, Justine?" Since she'd called on a first-name basis, he'd respond similarly.

"We have troubles here. Like that you found in the native population. Like the student's."

"Epilepsy?"

"Six of our techs are down. The automedic has them heavily sedated. One broke his thigh bone thrashing around."

"Did they come across another museum? Like the one here?" Ralston had visions of the physicists blundering about in the dioramas, experiencing the long-lost culture as Yago de la Cruz had done—and dying because of it.

"No." That answer chilled Ralston even more. The echoes from the past came back even stronger. He almost heard them creating chaos all around. "They tend to be the staff on planet the longest, however. Most of us are relative newcomers compared to them."

"I've been working on the assumption that the effects of the chaos device remained, even though the device itself went on," he explained. "The most obvious effects are the unpredictable weather and Alpha Prime going nova."

"It's a radiation rather than a poison? Can we shield against it?"

She approached the problem as a physicist. Block it out; keep working; study it later under controlled conditions. Chaos followed no rules.

"Is Bernssen all right?" Ralston asked, seeing Leonore's anguished face.

"Nels is as strong as a bull. Nothing stops him," came the gratifying answer. "But I have ordered a termination of all experiments over the next three days. Four days from now we lift for orbit. Conditions then will determine if we stay any longer or star for Novo Terra immediately. I thought you should know."

"Thank you, Justine. Is there anything we can do?"

"Our automedic isn't equipped to handle six at once. Can Nels bring three of the, uh, victims over so yours can care for them? You might have to shuttle them to your starship if things turn suddenly worse."

Ralston knew that conditions could only deteriorate.

"Bring them over. We can use Bernssen's help shutting down our own work."

"Michael, no!"

Ralston motioned Leonore to silence. The signal broke up continually and he strained to hear Justine Rasmussen.

". . . over right away. Look for him within a few hours. The mud plains are especially treacherous now."

"All right, Justine. Thank you again for the warning."

Ralston clicked off the com unit and sat, feeling curiously drained. All their work had been for nothing. The cloak of chaos had descended and hid knowledge from his eyes now.

"Michael, something's wrong."

"What?" He sat up, instantly alert. It took him several seconds to realize what it was. He relaxed again, as much as he could. "The rain's stopped. That's all."

"But the storm just started."

He tried to keep from screaming at her. What else did Leonore expect from chaotic behavior? It started, it stopped—at random. Their macroscopic world had become as indeterminate as the quantum mechanical domain. Anything might happen.

Anything.

FIFTEEN

"The sky's on fire," Leonore Disa said in a hushed tone. She stood at the base of the stairs leading to the alien museum, staring up at the dancing veils of lacy, electrical aurora. "The last time it was only white. Now I see reds and even blues and greens."

"Heavy ionization," said Nels Bernssen. He moved beside her, one arm circling her waist.

"It's so beautiful. I can hardly believe that this is the final performance."

"Curtain's coming down," agreed Bernssen. "You and Ralston about got your equipment packed away?"

"I told him it'd be all right to leave the supervisor," she said. "Daddy'll never miss it, especially if he gets some cut of the profits off the find. Michael agreed that since it was, in a way, IC's grant that got us back here in time, the company ought to have a minority share in any profits."

"Does that mean you've figured out the telepathy gadget? That'll bring in a planet's ransom in licensing fees."

"The licensing fees belong to the University. The monetary split will get nasty before everyone's finished. And no, we're still no closer to figuring it out, but Michael thinks he has a way of getting the information. He won't say how."

Leonore looked out at the desolate mud flats where they had packed a half dozen of the dioramas. They had taken tridee photos, run the analyzer for precise locations, had put all their data through the supervisor, done everything within their power to record in the hope of reconstructing on Novo Terra. But Leonore held little hope for that. The natives of Alpha 3 had been more clever than they. If only a full-scale expedition had been possible!

Engineers might have torn apart the displays and found the answer. Or xenopsychologists skilled with alien thought. Or any of a score of other researchers. She and Ralston were experts at uncovering, not figuring out how these devices worked.

And always the specter of the nova hung over them like the angel of death. There simply hadn't been adequate time to explore, to think, to try theory after theory until truth became obvious. No good science would be done on Muckup.

"It's starting to rain again," she said, pulling away from the museum door as a gust of wind stung her face. "Let's go see if Michael needs us."

"I want to check on the others," Bernssen said, worry creeping into his voice. "The automed doesn't seem to do very much for them. It pumps in tranquilizers but little else."

"If they've come down with what affected de la Cruz, there'll be neurological damage that can't heal." Leonore swallowed hard. "If we don't leave Muckup, we might all end up that way."

"How cheerful," Bernssen said, worry giving a brittle edge to his voice.

"How much longer?" came Ralston's shouted question. "As much as an hour?"

"The shuttle pod's ready to go within the hour," said Bernssen. "The last of the diorama crates needs to be loaded. The robots are working on them now, but the rain might slow them down. Call it two hours until launch."

"Good. As soon as the robots are finished with the important stuff, get them all here. I want the supervisor's full attention directed on this single diorama." Ralston pointed to one with four figures huddled around a low table. All stared at a blank sheet on the table as if it contained the wisdom of the universe.

"What's so important about this one?" asked Bernssen.

"Maybe nothing, but I'm betting everything on it being pivotal. The later ones"—Ralston pointed down the corridor to his right—"were obviously constructed within a few years of their eventual collapse. I feel those hold the most danger for anyone entering."

"Like de la Cruz," Leonore said in a whisper so low only Bernssen heard.

"This one seems to have been constructed after the object— what I'm calling the chaos device—passed but before the decline became obvious to everyone."

"You make it sound as if the people in this sideshow knew what it was," said Bernssen.

"I think that's true."

"But there's not enough time to study it. There are four figures. That," said Leonore, mentally calculating, "might be as long as ten hours of telepathic lessons."

Robots clanked down the corridor, some dripping chunks of mud. Ralston no longer cared. Within weeks or even days, the entire planet would be superheated vapor. Preservation of his find no longer mattered in the face of such cosmic catastrophe.

"All here?" Ralston asked. His face paled as he considered the danger in what he was about to do. He wobbled slightly and caught himself against the wall.

"Ready for dismantling, Michael." Leonore looked up from the remote panel. "Are you feeling all right?"

"Yes. Now listen carefully and don't argue. I want the entire display removed intact. Blast a hole through the roof and lift it out in one piece. Load it onto the shuttle immediately. Then I want you to gather anything important—don't miss a single block circuit!—and then get yourself and Bernssen's colleagues onto the shuttle."

"We can start them right now, if you like," said Bernssen. "That'd speed up the transfer."

Ralston wasn't thinking straight. All he wanted was assurance that this particular diorama reached orbit and the IC starship cargo bay intact.

"Do it however you like."

Leonore made a single adjustment to the remote panel. Outside, robots began shifting the anesthetized victims of the chaos device to the shuttle.

"You make it sound as if you won't be able to supervise," said Leonore.

"I've left my notes in the analyzer, if anything happens. I'm sure they won't blame you."

"What are you going to do?" Leonore asked sharply.

"As soon as I enter the diorama, begin removal."

"With you in it? Are you crazy?" Bernssen's shock turned his face into a flowing putty mask of confusion.

"I don't want to kill myself, but this means too much not to make one last try. If I activate the telepathic projection circuit, then you move the entire diorama, perhaps we can keep it intact until we get back to Novo Terra."

"Michael, this is ridiculous."

Leonore's protest fell on deaf ears. Ralston stepped forward, chose his subject, turned and assumed that posture. He reeled a bit as the mental projection took hold. He sensed a substantial difference in the "texture" of the thoughts, a definite indication of change from the earliest dioramas. Then he became lost in arcane discussions and melted into his role.

"He's lost it," said Bernssen. "I'll get him out of there and..."

"No!"

"Leonore, we can't ship him back like this. It might kill him."

"What's he got to lose, Nels? His life? That's a small price to pay if he learns how this device works. And if he returns to Novo Terra without it, what are they going to do to him?"

"The psychologists would get him," Bernssen said in a choked voice. "If they find him guilty of de la Cruz's death, they'll wipe his mind and rehab him."

"Which would you want?" Leonore asked.

In answer, Bernssen turned, pushed her away from the remote control panel, and began changing the settings. "I'm better at this than you are. More practice. And I've been here longer to learn to really hate the mud."

His words were drowned out by the sound of ultrasonic diggers working their way through the roof of the alien museum. In less than five minutes the diggers had chewed away a hole large enough to lift the entire diorama onto the rainy surface.

"Shouldn't we protect it from the rain?" asked Leonore.

"Being done now. The electrostatic field is being scrambled by the lightning and upper atmosphere ionization, but it ought to repel most of the rain." Bernssen played the remote like an organ, producing whines and hisses and hums from the toiling robots.

The robots in the corridor had been working on the dioramas to either side of the one where Ralston stood frozen, his eyes wide and his throat trembling as if he subvocalized. Another ten minutes passed before the robots demolished the dioramas around their target. Leonore cringed at the wantonness of that work, but she knew it was necessary.

Ralston's life might depend on it.

"We're ready to lift it now," said Bernssen. Leonore couldn't tell if sweat beaded his forehead or if raindrops blew through the roof and ran down his face. "Here it goes."

Leonore clapped hands over her ears and twisted away. Torn metal screamed as the robots lifted the entire scene. Bernssen worked constantly now, adjusting, making certain that the robots did not apply torque to the floor of the diorama.

"Get to the surface," Bernssen yelled over the whine of machinery pushed to its limits. "Make certain the robots aren't getting mired down."

Leonore raced to the stairs and hurried to the surface. The rain had slowed, leaving veils of fog intermixed with the sporadically falling drops. She began working as hard as any of the metal servants. The mud caused them to slide and turn out of position. She used manual overrides to correct, shouted instructions to Bernssen, worked as hard as if she lifted Ralston's diorama on her own back.

It finally slid away from the hole. The shrieks of tortured metal died. One robot fell to its side, treads spinning in opposite directions. Leonore turned it off. She felt as if she buried a friend. Patting it on the side of its block circuit case, Leonore quietly said, "Thank you," then turned her attention to the others.

"I'll use the main panel now," came Bernssen's voice. He had shut down the remote and worked directly from the master supervisor. The entire diorama began sliding over the mud flats and toward the spot where the exhibit might be loaded into the shuttle.

Two hours later, Bernssen and Leonore hugged one another, their job finished. "He's still in the diorama," Leonore said. "I put an analyzer in with him to monitor heart rate and respiration."

"Ralston's alive?"

"So far he's not showing any different response than in the other dioramas."

Bernssen began laughing. And the laughter soared to heights beyond his imagining, out of control, past human redemption. He heard Leonore's shouts as if they came from the end of infinity. Then the world went dark around him.

Nels Bernssen screamed and thrashed about. Disoriented, he struck out and found nothing.

"Calm down, Nels. Please!" Leonore's anguished voice returned a semblance of control to the physicist, and convinced him he hadn't suddenly died. He forced open one eye, then the other. For a few seconds he didn't recognize his surroundings.

It slowly penetrated. Weightlessness. He was in orbit. In a starship. Not his expedition's—Leonore's. Webbing held him so that he couldn't float off and hurt himself.

"What happened?" he asked. His voice turned gravelly in his throat and his mouth felt like a desert, complete with rocks and sand and slithering reptiles.

"You went a little crazy."

"Am I all right?" Fear welled within him. He panicked as much as Ralston had at the idea of the psychologists rehabilitating him.

"The ship's automedic says so. Some evidence of synaptic disorder, but that's beyond its capacity to diagnose."

"The chaos?""

Leonore nodded.

Bernssen flexed his fingers and toes, moved slowly, and decided he had full control of his extremities. He unfastened the web restraints; Leonore didn't try to stop him. He took that as a good sign.

"What about Ralston?"

"Still in the hold. I didn't want to disturb him until you could help get him out."

"You trust me not to go spacy on you?" He only half joked. He saw her expression and knew she trusted him with her life.

"Got to check in with Justine. She'll think I ran out on her."

"No need to worry over that. Here's a com unit. The pilot's been talking with your expedition pilot." She handed it to Bernssen.

"Call through to Justine Rasmussen, please," he said. Heavy static caused Bernssen to jerk the unit away. His ears rang from the onslaught. "You there, Justine?"

"We're off planet, Nels. You get away?"

"Verd. What's happening with our star?"

"It's got indigestion bad," came the answer. "We've sent out probes toward Novo Terra via rocket with automatic trips to shift them back as soon as the first wavefront hits. Don't know if it'll work, but we've got no choice. Our pilot says leave now or not at all. His equipment is showing anomalous readings due to radiation levels."

"What of our probes?"

"The ones into the star have all failed. No reason. They died long before they should have."

"Like Chen's did on the 1054," mumbled Bernssen, remembering what Ralston had told him.

"What?"

"Never mind, Justine. I hate to leave, but I think you're right. Alpha 3's ready to go bang."

"See you back on Novo Terra," the project leader said.

"Good luck, yourself." Bernssen turned off the com unit, glad to be rid of the incessant background static. To the pilot he said, "Get us back to Novo Terra. We may not have much time."

"Got to boost for at least a day. You know that, Doc. We got the time?"

"We'd better. There's no way of outrunning the wavefront from a nova. It'll be coming at us at the speed of light."

The pilot began his preflight preparations.

"Can't we just shift from here?" asked Leonore. "I know you're not supposed to do it within a half-dozen planetary diameters, but this isn't going to hurt anyone below."

"We need the proper velocity to start the shift," said Berns-

sen. "If we hit shift speed but aren't aimed right, we'll end up
in some out-of-the-way spot; if we aren't up to speed but are
aimed right, we'll fall short. So velocity is very important."

"The latter sounds better than going out in a flash," said
Leonore.

"Not if we ran out of air before we could recompute and
shift a second time. These are precise calculations." He snorted.
"That's why the pilots stay so aloof. They don't want to get
involved with their passengers and maybe miss something.
That's just superstition, of course, but they believe it—so it's
true."

Bernssen felt better putting his arms around Leonore and
holding her close.

"Let's get Dr. Ralston out of the diorama," she said finally.
"I don't like the idea of just leaving him there. Something
might happen when we star back."

"There's no telling where that projector's power comes from,"
agreed Bernssen. "Hate to permanently imprint him with the
alien history lesson and burn out everything else in his head.
That'd be as bad as rehabbing him."

They floated through a door and down the central axis to
the cargo bays. At Leonore's request, the pilot had kept them
at the same pressure as the rest of the ship. When they got
Ralston out, the pilot could reduce pressure to only a fraction
of a bar and give them that much more fresh air.

"Madre de Dios," murmured Bernssen. "He looks just like
one of the statues."

Leonore moved around the hold, looking at Ralston from
different angles. She hated to admit how close Bernssen's description came to reality. Ralston stood with that strange set to
his jaw. His throat muscles still worked, as if he swallowed
constantly, and his gray eyes were glassy and unfocused. But
Leonore felt a sense of life within the man, as if he understood
he had achieved all he'd hoped.

"How do we get him free?" asked Bernssen.

"I've never just walked in and pulled him out. I don't know
if the field would affect me, too." She longed to try it, to
experience what only Ralston—and Yago de la Cruz—had.
The life of an alien unfolded for her intimate perusal pushed
archaeology past the traditional boundaries and into unexplored
territory. And Leonore wanted to be a part of that exciting

pioneering effort, to feel the alien thoughts slide into her mind, take her back centuries, and instruct her as the young of Alpha 3 must have been.

"Let me try this." Bernssen swung a short length of rope and let it whip out to curl around Ralston's leg. A swift yank staggered Ralston, bringing him to his knees. For a moment his eyes failed to focus, but wonder slowly replaced the stupefied expression.

"I did it," he said softly. Louder, "I did it! The diorama is still functioning!"

Leonore helped her professor to his feet. His knees trembled and the paleness gave him the aspect of a corpse, but his triumph wasn't to be denied.

"We did it! Salazar will have to roll over and play dead now. The Alpha 3 find is the most significant ever!"

"Are you sure the sideshow gadget still works?" asked Bernssen. "You might have been a sort of human feedback circuit. Take you out and it dies."

"No, it can't be that way. I won't permit it to be that way!" Ralston jerked free of Leonore and stepped back into the diorama, taking another position. The familiar rictus took control and froze him into an attentive statue. Bernssen retrieved him once more using his makeshift lariat.

"Still works, eh?" Bernssen said.

Ralston's immense smile told the story. He grinned even more when he said, "I chose well. The history lesson in this diorama tells of—"

A raucous warning alarm cut him off. Over the cacophony came the pilot's anxious voice, "Get out of the cargo hold and into webbing. I'm depressurizing for immediate acceleration."

"What's going on?" demanded Ralston.

Neither Leonore nor Bernssen had any idea. As fast as they could, they pulled their way up the central shaft and into the lounge area. As they strapped down, Ralston flipped on the com unit. The datascreen showing the cockpit had already been turned on.

"What's wrong?" Ralston asked the pilot.

"Bad radiation surges. We're getting fried in orbit. If I try lifting us to a higher orbit before vectoring off for a shift, we'll be exposed even longer. We just passed behind the planet. Got to blast hard for our shift point. No time to talk."

Ralston watched the man working feverishly. Behind him he heard Leonore and Bernssen quietly talking.

Bernssen called forward, "I checked the remote probes I put outside on the ship. He's not exaggerating about radiation levels. The hull's protected us from a bad burn, but we can't last too long. The star's pre-nova. We may not have the time to get away."

"We will," Ralston said more confidently than he felt. "Do you have an analyzer working on the star now?"

"Of course. That supervisor getting left behind is a loss. Could have really used it, but we have enough analyzers around to gather the data I need. That Rayleigh-Taylor instability had worsened, over a fifty percent density difference in the inversion layer. That must be building up pressure internally. The sun's going to superheat, then explode past the denser material."

The pilot applied even more acceleration and slammed them back into their couches. Ralston changed the screen to show Alpha 3. A catch came to his throat as he looked down on the nightside of the planet. Brilliant auroral prominences arched outward, seemingly coming from Alpha 3's surface. Intense lightning flashes illuminated thousands of hectares of the normally dark landscape, turning it into momentary noon. Ralston imagined what the conditions must be on Muckup's surface now. Rain storms of unending intensity, winds strong enough to slash the flesh from human bones, the lightning that almost blinded, the very air coming alive with static discharge.

Alpha 3 died before his eyes. And along with it went virtually all of the avian civilization that had once flourished there.

Virtually all.

Ralston threw up his arms to shield his eyes when a hundred lightning flashes hit simultaneously.

"Put the damned filter on," came the pilot's querulous voice. "There. Mark 3 polarizer on. And don't try to get a view of the sun at all. Burn your optic nerves out all the way to your brainstem."

"I'll get good enough photos," came Bernssen's voice. "When we get back to Novo Terra, I'll show them to you."

Ralston nodded. He couldn't take his eyes off Alpha 3. The radiation storms smashing into the sunward side must have reached titanic proportions by now. And as soon as they passed from the planetary shield, they, too, would bear the full brunt of that mad burning.

"Keep arms and legs in tight. *Here we gooooo!*"

The acceleration caused Ralston to black out. When he fought back to consciousness, he thought he'd gone blind. It took several seconds to realize that the external camera viewing Alpha 3 had burned out. He switched back to the cockpit. The pilot strained against the invisible bonds he applied to them all.

"We're gonna make it. We are," the pilot said. Ralston thought he was trying to convince himself rather than his passengers. "That damned star's a goner." Muscles rippled across the visible portion of the pilot's arm as he reached out to touch another control.

The additional acceleration pinned Ralston as surely as if glasteel bonds had been applied. Through half-hooded eyes he saw the pilot cross himself. Ralston succumbed to the pressure against his chest. Mercifully, he blacked out again, his last thoughts on fierce fifty-thousand-degree Kelvin prominences from the star creeping up slowly on them.

SIXTEEN

MICHAEL RALSTON SCREAMED, his world locked in a nightmare of exploding light, searing heat, and infinite falling.

Falling?

He fought to regain his senses. The harder he struggled, the more tangled he became. Finally forcing himself to look, Ralston saw that the restraining webbing on the couch had come loose; he had become entangled to the point where circulation in his right arm had been cut off. He clumsily pulled himself free, then floated a few centimeters above the couch and marveled that he was still alive.

They had all survived.

Behind him, Leonore Disa tried to restore consciousness to Nels Bernssen. The physicist hadn't been properly strapped into his couch. From the unnatural angle of his right leg, Ralston guessed the man had one and perhaps several broken bones. Only weightlessness kept him from intense pain.

"I'll get the automedic," Ralston said.

"I sent a signal to it already," Leonore told him. "Wait a

few minutes. It's still tending the others. We didn't have them fastened down too well, either."

Ralston wiped the sweat from his forehead and his hand came away wet and red. He started, then relaxed. His head hurt like a son of a bitch, but the wounds were superficial. His vision wasn't blurred, no ringing in his ears, and he felt ... alive.

"I've done what I can for Nels," the woman said. She kicked against one of the couches and arrowed forward to Ralston. "Let me take care of that gash on your head. Something must have come flying through the lounge. I picked up a few scratches myself. We should have tied things down better."

Ralston winced when she applied an astringent. Leonore frowned at the wound, took the tail of his shirt and placed it directly over the wound.

"Press hard. Good. The automed will be done soon enough."

Ralston decided it didn't matter if his shirt got any bloodier. It was ready for the disposal.

"What about the pilot?"

"He's all right. He was ready for the acceleration."

"Are we all right?"

Leonore laughed. "We must be. Wait a minute." She went to the com unit and turned it on. The pilot's off-key singing came through. Leonore arched one eyebrow, as if saying, "See? We're fine."

Ralston called out, "What's our status?"

"That you, Doc? We made it off, right on the point. Good work, if I do say so."

"The star went nova?"

"Can't say but it sure looked like it was trying hard. We got a few fried circuits but nothing dangerous. I evacuated the cargo hold. Hope you don't mind. Didn't want any radiation leaking in, then ionizing the atmosphere there. Cascades like hell, you know."

Ralston swallowed hard. Would the airlessness affect his diorama? He hoped not.

"We're on course for Novo Terra?"

"What's wrong? You didn't want to go there? Of *course* we're on course for Novo Terra. I'm the damnedest, best pilot that ever lifted from a planet." The pilot went back to singing his bawdy ballad about shoreleave on a pleasure planet. Ralston flipped off the unit, glad for the silence.

"We made it," he said. "We really did." He let the shock work its way through his body then. The danger had passed and they were on their way home.

Back to Novo Terra. Back to the University of Ilium. And Salazar's committee and the de la Cruz family.

Ralston wondered if he had only traded one danger for another.

"The automedic's working on Nels," said Leonore. "I'll have it check you out next."

"Uh, thanks."

"We succeeded, Michael," she said softly. "It's all over."

"Over," he repeated dully. All Ralston could think of was the reception he'd get from Salazar.

"Is it safe?" demanded Leonid Disa. The chief executive officer and chairman of the board of Interstellar Computronics peered at the display skeptically. He heaved his huge belly up and braced it against the edge of the conference table as if readying himself for flight. "I'm not killing myself when the vidnews cameras come in."

"It's safe," Dr. Salazar assured him. "I've personally tried it. The experience is . . . unique."

Disa looked at his daughter, who nodded, then at Ralston. The archaeology professor said, "I've entered dozens of the dioramas with no ill effect."

"What of this de la Cruz boy?"

"That was an unfortunate accident," spoke up Salazar. "We are going to be in litigation over it for some time, I'm afraid. That will, of course, slow development of this find, but . . ."

Leonid Disa snorted and boldly stepped into the diorama Ralston had retrieved from Alpha 3. The man's expression froze and his eyes glassed over. Forty minutes later, he sagged slightly and stumbled from the alien scene.

"That's the damnedest, most remarkable thing I've ever experienced. Think of the possibilities. Schools. Military training. My company can do a complicated briefing in a fraction of the time it takes now. IC is proud to have sponsored the expedition that brought this back, Dr. Salazar."

"But the University owns it, Citizen Disa." Salazar's smooth reply told Ralston that this had been well thought out and had been decided they owned it since Ralston was an employee.

"You're forgetting where the equipment and money came from. And that was my daughter out there risking her life to bring this back." Leonid Disa shook his head. "IC owns this, Doctor."

"The terms of Dr. Ralston's employment preclude such an arrangement," said Salazar.

"A shame." Disa shook his head.

"Yes," agreed Salazar, delighted that the IC chairman had relented so easily. "But your quitclaim of the process will provide both financial and technical support for the University."

"I didn't mean IC was giving up the telepathy transmitter," said Disa. "I meant it was a shame that IC has to retract all its funding for this school. What's that total this year, Dr. Salazar?"

From the way Salazar turned pale, Ralston guessed it amounted to a sizable sum.

"Of course," said Salazar, trembling, "the University needs a corporate partner to properly develop and market this machine. IC might be the appropriate company."

"We'll license it." Disa named a ridiculously small sum. Salazar started to protest, then changed his mind.

"The lawsuit over Citizen de la Cruz's unfortunate accident . . ." Salazar said.

"We'll see about settling that. I know the de la Cruzes. Money-hungry upstarts. They'd sell their immortal souls if it fattened their credit balance enough. IC wants this, Dr. Salazar. We want it badly."

"Doctor, the newsers," came the worried secretary's voice. "Should I allow them in?"

"At once. Don't keep the vidnews waiting," Salazar said with gusto, again in his element.

Ralston thought he might be sick. Since they'd returned to Novo Terra, everything had been taken from his control. Salazar had pounced on the working diorama like a carnivore hungry for a meal. Still, Ralston hadn't minded too much. Salazar had postponed the proceedings against him in the de la Cruz death— and Ralston saw that Leonid Disa might take care of that matter completely.

Ralston sighed. It'd be good to return to a more routine schedule—and to pursue what he had learned on Alpha 3.

"Citizens," spoke up Salazar, "we are here today to announce the discovery of a device that will revolutionize education." Salazar went on to briefly describe the telepathic projector's discovery, function, and potential.

"Dr. Salazar, is it true that this device was whisked away from Alpha 3 just minutes before its star went nova?" The newser motioned to bring cameras in closer for the reply.

"It is. One of our very own graduate students, Leonore Disa, was responsible. She is the daughter of the chairman of Interstellar Computronics, and, uh, co-sponsor of this expedition." In a voice almost too low to hear, Salazar added, "She worked under the tutelage of Michael Ralston of our University."

"Citizen Disa, comments?" The newser elbowed Salazar out of the way. Leonore tried to speak, to give Ralston the credit for the discovery. When her replies didn't jibe with what the newser wanted, he quickly turned to Leonid Disa. The crusty industrialist had dealt with the news before; he gave them curt, slightly belligerent answers. They focused fully on him.

Salazar cut in. "We have begun intensive investigation of the mechanisms. Our Dr. Binton, head of the University engineering department, will be in charge."

"Binton?" asked Ralston in a low voice. "How'd he get into this?"

Leonore shrugged. "Salazar must have thought Binton had better camera presence than you."

"He ought to. All he does is lecture at women's clubs and write articles on how microwaves are your friend."

"Don't, Michael. Being bitter isn't going to solve anything."

He saw that Leonore was right. He'd been let off the hook and ought to be happy, but the discovery of a lifetime had slipped through his fingers. The engineering department now took full credit for the telepathic projector—or as much as Leonid Disa would let them. The elder Disa wanted his daughter to receive full credit for the discovery.

Ralston wasn't inclined to argue that point. Leonore had furnished the starship, the expensive equipment supervisor, and the personal support that had made it possible to recover the diorama from Muckup. Without her and her father's money, Ralston would have been left with nothing except headaches.

"Can we get away from this?" he asked her.

She pointed to a side door in the conference room. No one noticed their leaving. Binton, Salazar, and Leonid Disa held the newsers' cameras and attention.

"No one's mentioned the most important thing," Ralston said as soon as they were in a quiet room. "The *message* in the diorama confirms what I'd thought. They called it a comet. Apparently it was supposed to be intensely brilliant, but it wasn't. No tail, no coma, nothing. An astronomical flop."

"You feel it was the chaos device?"

"What else?" Ralston said, enthusiasm burning brighter now. He began to pace, hands behind him. "The time frames are perfect. This diorama was constructed approximately a hundred years after the passage of their under-achieving comet. These scientists, the ones depicted in the diorama, are worried about the rise in civil disorder—and epilepsy. Their fears are truly paranoid, without much foundation, but they are worried. *Were* worried."

"Do you think there's any danger of catching the epileptic breakdown from the diorama?"

Ralston impatiently shook his head. "Not really. Maybe. How can I say? Some vestige of the field remains on the planet. De la Cruz is dead, and six of the solar physics scientists are disabled. The weather patterns are chaotic. The sun's going nova definitely shows that the field affected the stellar furnace mechanisms, even if it came slowly. It took almost ten thousand years for its regular fusion cycle to be disrupted."

"But Nels and the others . . ."

"They were on Alpha 3 almost three times as long as we were. The lingering effect might be more intense in some places than at others. Who can say? We're dealing with forces of unknown power."

"The medics say Nels will be all right. A tiny chemical neurotransmitter imbalance, they said. That was all they could come up with to explain the seizure." Leonore heaved a heart-felt sigh. "His brain scans are normal now."

Ralston knew that the others who had been struck down weren't as lucky. All of them would be slightly impaired in movement, but their health would not be affected further now that they were away from the insidious presence of the chaos field.

Ralston almost laughed at himself. He thought of it as a field. It might not be a radiation at all. Maybe the earliest guesses made by the avian natives were right. Poison. Or some-

thing totally beyond their—and the Alphans'—ability to understand. But until he had more data on the phenomenon, he'd
continue thinking of it as a radiation device scattering chaos
to and fro.

"That clears up a lot that had been worrying me," he said.
"Nels and the others. Now we can concentrate on the real find."

"Real find? What's that? The diorama is being torn apart
by the engineering department."

"They're interested only in the projector. No one has questioned the meaning of what was transmitted. Those alien scientists didn't say it outright, but they implied that they were
beginning construction of a starship. I caught whispers of a
scientist named Dial. They considered him a crackpot, but I
believe he succeeded prior to the final decline."

"They didn't have the technology!" protested Leonore.

"Exactly. Without faster-than-light travel, they'd have to
launch a sublight ship. I think this Dial built the ship and
launched it. Maybe they left just a few years before their entire
civilization collapsed. Maybe it was at the last possible instant."

"It might not have left at all."

Ralston smiled and motioned for Leonore to follow. They
left the building and headed toward the laboratories.

"Where are we going?" Leonore turned and looked over her
shoulder at the administration building. "I'm not sure we ought
to leave yet. The newsers might . . ."

"They don't need us. The newsers have their story being
spoon-fed to them by Salazar—and we're not a part of it any
longer."

"Michael, I'm sorry about that."

"About what?" he said in surprise, his thoughts far distant.

"About their saying I'd discovered the dioramas. That was
your discovery, but they didn't give me the chance to correct
it. I know what it means to you."

Ralston shrugged it off. "Let them say what they want. After
this, Salazar will leave me alone, and we can pursue this to
the logical end. *That* will be a solution to rock them back."

"Finding the starship?"

He nodded.

They trooped up the stairs to the second floor. Ralston hesitated as he always did before the door to Westcott's lab. The
idea of entering made him uneasier than experiencing alien

thoughts blasted into his brain by the avians' telepathic projector. He heaved a quick breath, knocked, and entered.

Westcott sat in his chair, eyes half-closed, mouth slack.

"He's the one, isn't he?" said Leonore with some disgust. Her quick brown eyes darted to the authorization hanging on the wall. "He's plugged in directly to the computer."

"The only one allowed to do it at the University."

"So slow," murmured Westcott, drool running from the corner of his mouth. As a robot might, he reached up and methodically wiped it away. "I am so slow today. Can't integrate quickly enough."

"Westcott," Ralston said, too loudly. He moderated his voice. "Have you worked out the trajectories I gave you?"

"What? Oh, it's you." Westcott's rheumy eyes focused. No pleasure showed that he enjoyed their company. No displeasure came, either. He was a part of his machine. "An interesting problem. Where would a sublight spaceship go, given the astronomical parameters of the Alpha system ten thousand years ago?"

The entire wall at the back of the laboratory glowed a dull blue. Pinpoints appeared.

"This is the position of the stars ten thousand years ago. That," he said, indicating a flaming orange line, "is the vector of the chaos device."

Leonore started to speak, but Ralston silenced her.

"How did you determine its speed?" he asked the mathematician.

"Couldn't from the shoddy data given. But the information from the planet gave me several parallax sightings. From this I determined apparent motion. Coupled with distance estimates, I came out with the vector. Fast moving, not quite light speed but close."

"But the spaceship?" prompted Ralston.

"There." A single light flashed so intensely that Ralston and Leonore shielded their eyes. This was Westcott's moment of drama. The scene faded and he turned back to whatever imponderable problem he'd been working on when they entered his domain.

"But we need more," said Leonore. "Just a light on a datascreen doesn't—"

Ralston silenced her. He pointed to a hardcopy imprinter.

A single plastic sheet lay atop it. He picked it up, quickly scanned it, and then left Westcott's lab without even thanking the mathematician.

In the corridor outside the lab, Ralston leaned back against the wall and wiped away a sheen of sweat from his forehead.

"He bothers you, doesn't he?"

"He bothers everybody, but he's useful. No, more than that. He's a damned genius because he's linked to his computers. But that doesn't mean I have to like dealing with him. Let's get back to my office. I want to look this over more closely."

They walked out to the Quad, then stopped. Several demonstrations grew in intensity. One in particular caught Ralston's attention. He pointed.

"See the P'torra? And the gadget in his hand? That's an impulse driver. He's using it to gauge the mood of the crowd. Whatever it tells him, he passes along to the one haranguing the others." A woman stood on a small chair yelling incoherent phrases.

"She's saying something about God's will being ignored with the diorama," Leonore said, shocked.

"Come on. If the P'torra sees us, he'll focus the crowd on us."

"But the dioramas are such a potent hope for us. Just imagine! We can alleviate . . ."

"That's not the point. The P'torra wants only to hone his skill at rabble-rousing. Actually, I suspect he'd love to be able to steal the telepathic projector. He might be promoted all the way to the top of the military pyramid."

"He's a soldier? I thought that only their students were allowed on campus."

"What's the difference? To them there isn't one. Come on before they see us."

Ralston climbed the steps to his office in silence. The P'torra provided a constant source of irritation for him. But between the P'torra and the newsers, he wasn't sure who he hated more. The newsers sought only the momentary thrill, the brief scandal, whatever titillated. He had a solid story for them.

An entire race had been destroyed by a force—artificial or natural?—passing through space near their planet. The culture had collapsed, their solar system had been destroyed by their G-class sun going atypically nova. A single spaceship containing their leading scientists might have escaped almost ten thousand years ago—and he held their most probable destination in his hand.

Did the newsers care about that? No, they gobbled up the muck that Salazar fed them about a trinket. Granted the projector from the diorama might be a profitable and useful gadget, but it meant less than finding the remnants of an entire civilization.

Or the device that had destroyed it.

Ralston closed the door behind Leonore and dropped heavily into his own chair. He pressed the switch for the projector.

"There it is," he said. "I'm going to call it Beta, for lack of a better name. That's where they fled for sanctuary when they left Alpha 3. I know it."

Leonore stared at the datascreen, then said, "You sound so positive about what happened. You can't be, even with what you learned in the last diorama."

"All the data fit into a matrix. This is the answer. The only one that makes any sense. The avian natives fled their dying planet, and we're going to follow."

"Will the University let you?"

Ralston laughed harshly. "They'll be more than happy to get rid of me for however long it takes. Out of sight, out of mind. I disturb their neat, orderly society."

"You force your students to think," Leonore said.

"That's what I just said. I disturb the current order at Ilium." Ralston flipped over to another screen of data. "If the University won't fund this expedition, do you think your father might?"

"What? Why, I suppose so, if I ask him. But IC isn't known for such funding ventures. He'll be hard-pressed to justify it to the board of directors."

"No, he won't." Ralston smiled without any humor. "Not when you tell him we'll bring back someone who can construct one of those projectors. I don't think Binton will be able to reverse-engineer the device. Not soon."

Leonore laughed. She enjoyed the irony of this. "You really think we can find the survivors of Alpha 3, get them to license it, and return before anyone can build a duplicate?"

Ralston nodded.

"That's rich. And with them in the spotlight, they'll take the heat for it, too."

"Archaeology has its moments," Ralston said. "But I'm more concerned about one other problem."

"What's that?"

"The chaos device. It's still out there. And it might still be actively interfering with the natural processes of the universe. Can we afford to let such a weapon be held at our heads?"

"You're exaggerating, Michael."

He didn't think so.

"Things turned out well enough for us this time. What if the chaos device comes back? By Novo Terra? We're not immune. Yago de la Cruz showed that. The members of Justine Rasmussen's research team proved it, too. We've got to find it and destroy it."

Michael Ralston started planning the new expedition to Beta with Leonore, but the thought burned like a black flame inside his head: The chaos device might destroy them all. And only he believed enough in the danger it posed to attempt to stop it.